small stations fiction

Suso de Toro

Tick-Tock

Published in 2016 by
SMALL STATIONS PRESS
20 Dimitar Manov Street, 1408 Sofia, Bulgaria
You can order books and contact the publisher at
www.smallstations.com

This book was first published in the Galician language as *Tic-Tac* by Ediciones B (Barcelona, 1993) and in Galicia by Edicións Xerais de Galicia (Vigo, 2003). This translation follows the Xerais edition. The black-and-white photographs in this book are from the Galician edition and are the combined work of Suso de Toro and Tino Viz. A list of our fiction titles can be found at www.smallstations.com/fiction.

This work received a grant from the General Secretariat of Culture of the Ministry of Culture, Education and University Planning of the Xunta de Galicia in the call for translation grants of the year 2015.

Esta obra recibiu unha axuda da Secretaría Xeral de Cultura da Consellería de Cultura, Educación e Ordenación Universitaria da Xunta de Galicia na convocatoria de axudas para a tradución do ano 2015.

ISBN 978-954-384-056-4

Suso de Toro

Tick-Tock

Translated from Galician by **Jonathan Dunne**

Small Stations Press

Contents

Third Sorrowful Mystery
THE TYRANNY OF DNA   123

Fourth Sorrowful Mystery
USURY AND CONSTIPATION, ASEPSIS AND STERILITY   163

Fifth Sorrowful Mystery
THE BOGEYMAN'S WORK   211

For Mariña, for when she's much, much, much older

For Antonio and Mercedes, and in memory of my grandparents

First Sorrowful Mystery

THE BOGEYMAN'S PROPHECY

What weather, eh. The day's got off to a good start. It doesn't stop; once it starts raining, there's no stopping. Before that, we all used to cry out for rain, saying there's a drought, the plants are drying up, in the winter the mountain will burn, and stuff like that. Now, there's rain for you. Take that. By the way, I like the rain, eh, careful now; if I don't have any for a while, it feels like I'm missing something. What would happen to us, we who are like grass, without rain? The other thing rain does is it makes you more aware of the passage of time, you feel it more, so to speak. That's true, as true as the fact time passes straight through us, carrying bits of us away. Just like that. I sometimes think I can feel it passing straight through me. Especially when it rains. That's right, ho, rain teaches us that life means losing bits of us all the time. There we go, now I've got all nostalgic and started philosophizing. As soon as it rains and I let my guard down, bam, I'm off philosophizing. Though let me say I don't dislike this fact. Positively. But when it's been raining for several days, like this, I have the impression I can't breathe, I'm drowning. Something gets inside me, right down inside, and takes over all the time. A kind of nostalgia, or melancholy, something like that. When it gets like that, I think about the Amazon River in Brazil and how sunny it must be over there right now, it's a lot to think about. I also remember when I was a child, it was very sunny back then. Spring would arrive, and in summer it would get pretty sweltry... Not any more. They say it has nothing to do with the fact the Americans went to the Moon, but I think it does. Of course, there are folk who are a whole lot more scientific than me, but I don't care. They should never have gone to the Moon. After all, what the hell did they do it for? I wonder who could explain it to me, because I don't know. Boh, doesn't matter. Let it rain. After all, there's no way of getting everyone to agree; if I want sun, the other wants rain, and vice versa. By the way, vice versa means back to front – if I want rain, the other wants sun. That's vice versa for you. We're always doing vice versa, whatever we do. Especially when it comes to the weather. I remember when I was a child, with the weather this never used to happen. If it rained, well, it rained. But now we see the weatherman or weatherwoman on TV – it's like they're the ones who deal out and decide the weather – and off we go, all wanting sun. No, no, give me a couple of clouds, the sun hurts my eyes. People now, when it comes to the weather, act like they're in the butcher's or a clothes shop. Like that sister-in-law of mine, who works in a clothes shop and is always saying, 'Every client that comes in through that door, I'd have them shot,' that's what she says. She's a bit bad-tempered, but then again, it's what she says, every client that comes in wants to see every article of ladies' underwear she has, they only sell women's clothes in that shop, it's a lingerie shop, they sell corsetry, bras, you wouldn't believe... whenever I pass in front of one of those lingerie shops, I can't believe some of the articles on display... oh, goodness. I sometimes stand there with my mouth open, of course you can't touch even if you wanted to, the window's in the way, and I stare at all those busts with their lace brassieres... The bust is the body part that comprises the breasts and shoulders. I see those busts and those brassieres... Oh, goodness me. And though one would like to maintain control of the situation, well, sometimes it gets difficult. Once this saleswoman came outside to tell me off. 'Off with you, you great big brute.' I wasn't doing anything, I was just looking, I'm not a pervert, it's normal if you're looking to have your hand in your trouser pocket. I don't see what's so bad about that. Begging your pardon. What to say, some people are very misunderstanding, I was just looking at what was on display, which is what it's for, right. Begging your pardon. A little comprehension, for goodness' sake, we're all made of flesh, that woman too, and flesh is like everything else, it doesn't last. There are times one feels somewhat misunderstood. One wants to be as one should be. I always wanted to be what others expected of me, but one never gets it right. I always have the impression someone or other is laughing whenever you get it wrong. Then I learned it doesn't matter, it's better to do your own thing, but it takes several years. How is one supposed to do what others expect? That's always been my problem, not getting it right. Even though you're always paying attention, how should I behave towards this guy, what should I do with that girl, careful what you say... Forget it, it's really difficult. Positively. One wishes to please. But no way. I'm not asking for much, just a little comprehension. But people are very misunderstanding. Positively. Begging your pardon. Better not to think about certain things; if you start thinking about this and that to the end, well, my friend... I don't know what it is with these days of rain, the sadness gets right inside you. Either that, or it was already inside you, and when it rains, out it comes. Vice versa. It must be that, it's already inside you, lurking in its lair, and when the opportunity arises, tap-tap, out it comes, front feet first, tap-tap. It must be that. What other things must be lurking inside? The further down you go, the more things there must be. Positively. But of course there's no way of getting all the way down inside. I read the other day the Japanese have invented a gadget that goes all the way down inside, reads your thoughts and brings everything out into the light of day. Like you're a well or something. Progress is good, but I have to say such things make me feel a bit afraid. Unless it's a joke, some prank by a journalist who didn't have anything else to write about, so he came up with a new invention. 'Breikhead' it was called, I think that's what it was. With a 'k'. Though it may have been 'brakehead' or even 'braikehead'. Something like that. Better not to think about it; if you think about it too much, it sends a shiver down your spine. One always wants to know what's down there, inside, but that said, I wouldn't let anyone go peeping around. You let them bring all of that outside, everything you've got hidden inside you, and there won't be anything left. No way. It's like... I don't know, like you've stopped being you, you're not needed any more. That's it, you've been stripped of all your mystery. Don't need you, throw him away. Like you're an empty beer can. You've nothing left to tell. No way. Not even as a joke. After all, even though one is here without having asked to be, all the same, one wants to decide one's own life. One wants to know what's deep down inside, who knows what mysteries would turn up? Each person is a universe. But to let everybody see it, for all of that to appear on a screen, so that anyone can watch it, like it's a film, no way. Nowadays people just want to know it all, to see it all. None of that. We can't allow that to happen. I understand we all have a vested interest, I get that. But doing it's another thing. There has to be a little mystery. It's one thing to stave off your hunger, another to stuff yourself to the brim. No siree. If someone wanted to have a peep with that gadget thing, they'd have to pay me. You betcha. I wouldn't do it for a million or two. Or for a bet, either. Five million, and we could talk. Or more, twenty million. Then I'd grab the money and take a trip to the Amazon. Or buy myself a villa and swimming pool in Majorca. Wouldn't you just love a sunny villa, taking a dip in the pool and watching planes fly overhead? When it rains like this, all the time, it's better to think about sunny places, otherwise you can get all nostalgic, all lonely... That's because we have a heart. Though there are folk who don't have a heart, and they're the happiest. A cousin of mine, named Fernando, is the biggest bastard that will fit inside your head. Think of the biggest bastard you know. I mean big, big. Go on, think of him. Thought already? Even more. My cousin Fernando is even more of a bastard. And I say that despite the fact he's a cousin of mine. Truth be told, Fernando is a nasty piece of work. He has the blackest innards I know. Even though his mother, my aunt Moncha, is as good as gold. She'll give you everything she has. That son of hers finished her off.

I reckon it was Fernando who gave her cancer. Cancer doesn't just come along; if you're working and healthy, your husband loves you, your son behaves, then you don't just go and catch cancer. Goodness me, this son of theirs wanted to sell the house with them inside it. Of course, if he's hooked on drugs... I don't mean pills, I mean syringes. The money doesn't stretch that far. So one day a married couple turns up on the doorstep of my uncle and aunt's house, wanting to see it. You must be joking. My uncle asks why don't they go and see the house of the slut who bore them? My uncle Paco, he can really fly off the handle. Well, the others, they asked wasn't this the house and garden that were up for sale? My poor aunt, she felt terrible. And I reckon that's when she got breast cancer. But just imagine what my cousin Fernando is like, he's never had a problem getting to sleep. Do you think, having got up to one of his tricks – and some of them have been pretty bad – he had trouble going to sleep? Uh-uh. Never. The guy was a real demon, but he slept like an angel. Like an innocent. So listen to this: the less of a person you are, the better you sleep. Otherwise, just look at animals, they never have trouble going to sleep. Or look at that guy Maquieira, a police inspector who was crippled after a severe beating. Well, his soul was blacker than coal, but I always remember him in the Floyma, Florentino's place, sitting at a table and dozing off. Sleeping at all hours. Some people are just like animals. If you're a real person, you always feel a bit guilty; whether you like it or not, there's always something going on. And sometimes quite a lot. So if you're a real person, you feel guilty, and that guilt disturbs your sleep. Children also suffer from insomnia. Children, you see, they also have their little problems. We like to think, just because they're children, they don't have any problems, but they do. Not long ago, I went to have dinner at my sister's house – I sometimes do that, you know – and after dinner I crept into my nephew Iván's room and found him all huddled up under the blankets, with only his eyes showing. The light was on, but there he was, all terrified, his eyes wide open. I knew what he was afraid of, of course: the Bogeyman, the Sack Man. He was afraid, when he heard footsteps and the door opened, it wouldn't be his uncle Nano, but a man with a knife. 'What is it, Iván? Can't you sleep?' I asked. 'No,' he says. 'Why's that?' I ask. 'I'm afraid,' he says. 'What of?' I ask. 'Ugly things,' he replies. Trouble is these days they watch so much television, all sorts of nonsense, I've no idea how they get to sleep. That said, there wasn't so much telly before, but we children were still afraid. When you think about it, there's no doubt children have real problems. I wouldn't want to be a child, no siree. They'd have to pay me for it. I wouldn't be a child even if they paid me a million or two. They'd have to pay me ten million at least, or fifteen. Fifteen, and we could talk about it. With fifteen million as a child, you could have yourself a pretty nice childhood. Of course, unless there's understanding and affection on the part of the adulterers, then that's not worth much either. Money without understanding and affection isn't worth a great deal. It really is pretty difficult to be happy. Though, that said, there are some who are afraid and don't say anything about it, but I do. At night-time, I'm sometimes afraid the Bogeyman will come. Because I've seen him, I have, the Bogeyman. You listen first, then express your opinion. The first time was several years ago, I wasn't a child any more. One day, I catch sight of this guy with long hair and a straggly beard, wearing a raincoat down to his knees, I have a good look and see he's following a girl who's just left school with her satchel. So I go after them. And at this point, I don't know how, the guy opens his raincoat, and out comes a huge knife that's just hanging there. I start to shout, 'Hey, you, listen,' things like that. And of course people look over at us, the guy takes to his heels and disappears. Then the people start looking at me, as if to say, 'This guy's off his head,' but the other, he knew what was going on and disappeared. It was the Bogeyman. I've seen him a few times since then, wearing different clothes, he likes to get dressed up. Once, I turn around and realize he's following me down the street. I look, and there he is, dressed up as a priest, I can tell it's him from the face, you don't forget that face so easily. It's him, and he's coming for me. I start running, jump on a passing bus and leave him behind. 'I'll catch you when you're dead,' he shouts. People act as if nothing's happening. When I recall that incident, I get goose pimples. That's the fear I carry inside. Fear he'll catch me before then, but also fear he'll be waiting for me on the other side. I'm quite certain what follows this life is the Bogeyman. But you can't say things like that, they'll laugh at you. If I could warn the whole world, inform people, then perhaps we could all be saved. If people were warned, there'd be a way we could catch him between ourselves and do him in. Perhaps then children, and the whole of humanity, would be saved. That said, I had a dream it's the boys and girls he likes best. But when I go telling people this, they just laugh at me. What people want is for you to tell them things they can believe; if you tell them things they can't believe, they don't like it and get annoyed. Besides, I have my doubts, he may have come out of my dreams; you know, if you dream something a lot, with all your strength, that thing can come to life and finish you off. Were it something good, that wouldn't matter, of course. Positively. But no, this thing isn't good. That said, I don't think he's the product of my dreams. If you want my opinion, he's the one who's behind all of this. The Great Schemer, the Great Troublemaker. He's the one who keeps watch from afar and from close up. Even though you can't see him, he can see you, and even though you don't know, he does. That's why you always have to be on your guard. Of course, if you're always on the lookout, then you lose your innocence and stop being a child. That's a real tragedy. I was lucky because I kept my innocence for a long time, my mother says I'm still an innocent. But I don't listen to her. Though she may be right, and that's why I keep seeing the Bogeyman out and about. You can't go around saying this stuff, people will make fun of you. It's better to talk about something else, not to embitter your life. This weather's really pretty awful. If only it would clear up a little, let the sun peep through. I just wish I could be in the Amazon River, or in that pool by my villa on a sunny day, or back in the village, in my grandparents' house, when I was little. Positively.

It Was Not Me (Go On, Cry)

'Ask my pardon.'

   'What for?'

   'For what you did, and because I tell you.'

   'I don't want to.'

   'Ask my pardon.'

   'No.'

   'Get down on your knees and ask my pardon. That's right, on your knees.'

At Nightfall

I'm in the pool, inside the water, holding on to the side with both hands. I hear the sound of a plane, lift my eyes and follow it across the expanse of sky. It disappears behind some buildings. I think of the people travelling somewhere on that plane. Going, or coming back. I feel a slow sadness as my body floats in the still water.

I let go and swim the length of the pool. Then I come back, again and again. Twelve times, I force myself to cross the blue water. I grab hold of the metal steps, almost at the end of my strength, and get out of the pool, feeling breathless. I come to a halt at the shallow end and, with the little strength I have left, launch myself head first against the bottom. I feel the bone cracking on the tiles, the blue chlorine entering my mouth, as my head goes cold. Up above, bluish clouds, and the water turns red. My body hangs limply in the water with wide open eyes.

As always with these things, it's at nightfall.

Old Isidro

If you wanted to do and be something in life, reaching old age isn't easy. It's not easy to see how the time has gone and you're still the same. All those years, you've been the same, fearful, weak and, deep down, pathetically ridiculous. To see yourself naked, in all your ridiculousness. Why didn't you have the humility to have no pretensions? Behind would be a life replete with sensible actions, the right gesture at each juncture. Ordinary things are the only that exist, they would have given you part of their rounded existence. All that exists is what is before you at each moment. But you couldn't see that, Isidro. Your myopic gaze slipped stealthily over the objects and places you encountered, keeping you permanently isolated from them, sheltered in the resting pavilion of words. Bleary words laboriously scrawled on pieces of paper, year after year. How cold, Isidro. In the end, what are all the words you thought, said and wrote worth if you don't have a child to name you, Isidro, to give clear, circular sense to your name, Isidro, pretentious trisyllable? Are they worth a dog's dinner? A little, humble dog, a mongrel that barks and wags its tail in contentment when it sees you approach. Ah, Isidro, they're not worth a barking dog's dinner. Look around at shelves crammed with books, files, the table covered in papers, all so familiar, so *heimlich*, and yet suddenly so sinister, so hostile, so *unheimlich*. So full of death. Don't blame the papers, you knew you were a taxidermist of words. What were you planning to leave as an inheritance except for scarecrows of words? It's difficult to confront this perspective of fragile paper architectures erected over almost fifty years with the dedication and devotion of a goldsmith from the height of your old body, thin legs and brittle bones, the hump on your back, the white hair poking out of your nose and ears, so large after the passing of years.

It's easy for tears, so rare in old age, to appear, decomposing the carefully constructed mask of dignity. The worst thing is you know they're the same tears, they taste the same, as when you woke up at night as a child and there was no one at home. Mother and father were out at the theatre. That's the worst thing, you acted the fool all your life for nothing, and now you've woken up, you're afraid, and no one is going to say your name so you can settle down and sleep peacefully. Sleep, Isidro, sleep. No, mother's not here. You've gone through all these years, and now you're naked, fearful and cold, as in the beginning. And mother's not here.

(Manuscripts of ISIDRO PUGA PENA)

ISIDRO PUGA PENA (1918-1988). Fiction and essay writer. One of the men who underpinned cultural activity in our country during the last forty years. Close to the circle of university people in the Seminary of Galician Studies, he combined interesting literary work with rigorous philosophical reflection.

In the year 1936, he published his first book, a short poetry collection, *Half Voice*. After the war and a period of exile in France, Argentina and Mexico, he returned to Galicia and, in 1958, published *Yes, No and Other*

Negations, a book of philosophical thought. In the 1960s, he published the best of his fiction – *Dark Furrow*, *Gestures in the Night* – and, in 1977, the novel *Great House*. He carried out a translation of Heidegger's work *Being and Time*, which remains unpublished.

He spent the last years of his life in a rest home, after attempting to take his own life. In his final winter, he suffered a grave crisis, gouging out his eyes and refusing to utter a word after that. He died of a brain tumour on January 10, 1988.

The texts we reproduce here, by kind permission of the legatee, belong to manuscripts from the author's final years. They reflect some of the recurring themes in his essays and fiction. Despite the ravages of illness, they still preserve the introspective rigour and painful intellectual implacability of his finest moments of prose.

Ithaca Perhaps

'Keep Ithaca always in your mind,' read Odysseus on the sardine tin, under the image of a bearded man with a sailing boat printed in the background. With these words, the memory came back to him, intense and clear. The white house glinting in the sunlight, between olives trees and the smells of cattle and work, the scents of honey and wine. He'd been away from home for a long time, and Ithaca was calling to him. He could hear his wife summoning him from afar. 'Odysseus,' she cried. He could make out the games of his child, Telemachus, and the barking of his dog, Argos. Yes, it was time to return. He should head north. Set out for home, Ithaca.

On the way, he continued amassing memories. Recollections of labours, parties at home, the bedroom, hunting in familiar hills... 'Ithaca,' he murmured. He allowed the word to linger on his lips, drawing out the taste of friendly things. He grew more and more anxious to arrive.

He moored the boat to the wharf; the harbour and streets were unknown to him. He asked the sailors lugging barrels of wine and crates of mackerel in brine for directions to his house. They pointed to a strange street. He hired a taxi to take him there. When it stopped in front of the gate, he didn't recognize the house. He knocked at the door, and Penelope opened, looking changed. This frail, mature lady was not the woman he'd left behind. He entered and bumped into a young man leaving with a helmet in his hand. He turned around to see him mounting a motorbike.

'Telemachus,' he called, 'it's me, your father.' But the boy didn't hear because of the roar of the engine.

That night, he looked out of the window to see the stars in all their blackness. He gazed at the garden, glimpsed in the shadows the grave of his dog, which had been run over by a lorry two years earlier. How, in the night, to distinguish one shade from another? 'Tomorrow I'll fix the compass. Where it shows north is the south. Then I'll leave.' This place wasn't his house, the one he'd left behind, he said to himself. This wasn't how he remembered it. 'Nothing is ever what it was. Nothing. Ever,' he thought before falling asleep. Nothing. Ever.

It Was Not Me (Go On, Cry)

'I don't want to.'
   'Ask my pardon.'
   'Pardon me for being so rude.'
   'Not like that. Ask properly.'
   'It was not me, it was my food.'
   'Either you ask my pardon, or you'll get into trouble.'

The Sea

After several hours of travelling by bus, the glass was misted over and, even though he'd wiped his hand and the tip of his raincoat over the glass to clean it, he was afraid the humidity would stop him seeing the sea when it appeared.

Five minutes earlier, Don Pepe had announced the nearness of the sea: 'There are five kilometres to go until we reach Foz.' He had spent those five minutes squeezing the plastic bag on which could be read 'Paqui Shoes, Becerreá', where he kept a cheese sandwich, a chorizo sandwich and a banana. For the last five minutes, he hadn't heard the racket of the other boys and girls who were excited at the sea's proximity. He had sat rigid and still, clinging to the plastic bag on his knees and gazing out at that landscape of pines, eucalyptuses and maize. Soon the sea would appear and, if he wasn't careful, he would miss it when it did. At his side, Bird, his best friend, had given up talking to him and was now laughing, looking at Mill two seats in front, who was shielding his face with his hand and shouting, 'Ship ahoy!' Next to him, Margarita of Bernal was waving her arms about, 'Help, captain, we're drowning!'

It was enormous. 'Vast,' Don Pepe had said, pointing to the blue expanse on the map. And green – blue and green. He had seen it on the telly. It stretched further than from the school to Piornedo, further than Becerreá, than two trips to Becerreá. Further than the eye could see, even were you to cross the mountains, further still.

Much further than Lugo even. It was enormous. And you could board a ship and go all around the world without stopping. It never finished. And it was very pretty; it had a terrible temper, sometimes it would get all worked up and create enormous waves. There were gigantic octopuses in its depths. And huge whales. His uncle had told him if you spent a lot of time at sea, you got seasick, as he did when he first set foot on board, but it was so pretty and so big he still wasn't tired of travelling on it. *He* wasn't going to get sick. Now, now. There it was, there it was. Over there. The sea.

The children started pointing and shouting, 'Over there! Over there!' It was the sea. Then they gradually fell quiet, their mouths and eyes wide open.

It was a blue object, far away, covering the horizon. All of it, salty water. It went on and on until it reached England. The boys started playing tricks again, shouting and causing mayhem. But he didn't hear a thing. Bird tugged his arm in order to say, 'It's a lot of water, isn't it?' But he hardly heard him, he smiled a bit and went back to looking through the window at this blue stain that was also green and was getting inside him, taking control of everything.

The road now passed between the first houses in the town. The children made even more noise. Shops, bars. 'Look at that house. There's the harbour. What a lot of booooooats!'

The bus moved alongside the breakwater, next to some towering piles of fish crates, and parked. The children's shouts grew in intensity, their little bodies trembling as if they had the shakes. 'Quieten down, everybody,' Don Pepe said a few words. 'No one is leaving until you've all quietened down.' Eventually, they fell silent. 'Good, now grab your bags of food, and let's go and see the harbour. I don't want anyone approaching the water, the sea is very treacherous. It's carried away far bigger, stronger men than you. Anyone who doesn't listen or gets wet is in for it. And don't go far, stay where I can see you. You've been warned. Does everybody understand?' 'Yeeees,' said Ferreira and Cacharro, and one or two others at the back, the rest just nodded with a solemn expression and great conviction. 'OK then, slowly and without pushing, you can get off. Careful now, I don't want anyone getting into trouble.'

The driver opened the doors, and Don Pepe emerged first. The children descended the steps, while the teacher warned them from the bottom, 'No boarding the boats, they all have an owner. Walk about, look around and behave. I don't want people saying, just because you're from the mountains, you're not proper people. Don't hurt yourselves and don't break anything.' Bird went down first and called out to him, 'Come on, Suso, get a move on!' Suso went down slowly, his eyes on the sea. 'Careful, Suso, keep an eye on the steps, otherwise you're going to fall,' said the teacher. 'They won't sleep tonight, they're so excited,' he remarked to the driver.

The two boys started walking along the wharf, feeling the wind, but oblivious to the cold of that chilly spring morning. There it was, all full of water. They went up to the edge and peered over at the water being rippled by the wind.

'It's a lot of water, isn't it?' said Bird.

'Sure, and isn't it pretty?' replied Suso. 'What things do you think there are deep down, at the bottom?'

'Fish, I suppose.'

They gazed out at it. They could see a few fish swimming along the bottom.

'Look, look. Trout,' said Bird.

'They're not trout, my uncle said there aren't any trout in the sea.'

'What are they, then?'

'I don't know, but they're not trout.'

'Come on, let's go.'

The other children were scattered all over the wharf, examining the boats, the heaps of baskets, sprawling on the nets.

'They sure can fly high, those seagulls. And they know how to hover, just like kites,' said Bird.

'That's right,' replied Suso, staring at the sea.

A huddle of boys and girls gazed in amazement at a woman darning the nets. She was sitting, barefoot, on top of the tackle, the wooden needle coming and going in her hands, as she laughed at the children. 'What is it, my darlings, where are you from?' Bird went up to the group. 'Come on, look!' he said to Suso. But Suso carried on walking slowly, his gaze fixed on the sea, which he could glimpse further on, where the breakwater ended. There, he'd be able to see the sea in all its entirety. The sea that never finished would start from there. The eternity

Don Santiago talked about would be like the sea: vast and never-ending. Like the Infinite, as Don Pepe said when he drew an eight lying down on the blackboard and said a number was forever. So broad, so broad it had no end. He walked with his raincoat open, flapping in the wind, clinging to the plastic bag with his sandwiches and banana in it.

It Was Not Me (Go On, Cry)

'Pardon me for being so rude.'

'You're going to get into trouble. Ask me properly.'

'It was not me, it was my food.'

'I said you'd get into trouble, didn't I? Didn't I say you'd get into trouble? Didn't I say so? Well, take that, then! And that!'

Steaks of the World

She wasn't concentrating on her driving. Every day, the same route, eight kilometres of cars and traffic lights. Every blessed day. And what for? She felt like packing it all in. She stopped at a light behind an old 2CV. Some 2CVs were still going. They were pretty resistant. How happy Ramón and she had been when they'd bought theirs. They'd celebrated the fact by driving to Finisterre. If only she could go back – they could go back – to being what they'd been then. Before Maruxa was born. Not even that. She didn't have the strength, or the will, to be Ramón's girlfriend again. Or to be anyone's girlfriend, when it came down to it. The 2CV pulled away slowly. The mist spattered the windscreen. She switched on the windscreen wipers once and could see. She turned on the sidelights, the morning was rather gloomy. It would probably clear up around midday. Besides, when they'd got married and driven around in the 2CV, they'd been a couple of youngsters. My goodness, how naive they had been. They were just like children. But they'd certainly laughed a lot and had a good time. Ramón had been very funny, great fun. He'd made her laugh again a month earlier, on New Year's Eve. Old jokes, she knew them already. But for a moment he'd sparkled the way he used to. Life had got so serious. Life really could be sad and boring. Get pregnant, give birth, breastfeed, change nappies, raise a daughter until she decides she wants to be independent, and then it seems she's against you. You've reared an enemy. Pay for an apartment, a bank gobbling up all your funds and life for years on end. At least Ramón applied for head of department, I didn't do anything. I should have specialized years ago, but raising a child and working is tiring enough, without having to study on top of that. She was tired, fed up, she felt like upping and leaving. After all, nobody would miss her. They had a maid to do the cleaning. Their daughter cooked when she felt like it, and her father would probably feel pretty content with only his daughter and position as head. He'd soon find somebody else. She felt like laughing. She came across a red light. The 2CV was still in front. The light changed, she continued. Hey, she'd just missed the turning for work. What a muddle she was in today! Now she'd have to carry on, to find somewhere to turn around. Back to work. Then lunch at home; by the time she arrived, the other two would have eaten. He'd be watching telly in the sitting room, and she'd be in the bathroom or her bedroom. She'd prepared the rice the night before and left a couple of breaded steaks; when they arrived, all they had to do was fry them. Blasted steaks and rice. The cars were moving more quickly now. She put her foot on the accelerator. She started laughing as she drove up the steep road. It seemed the mist was finally lifting, the warehouses were becoming more spaced out, giving way to fields and allotments as the day brightened and the sun came out. She wound down the window and switched on the radio. Blasted steaks of the world. There was a roadwork sign on one side. 'Road Closed in 2 Kilometres'. She had to turn around. She'd be late for work.

The Happiest Day

It's the happiest day, *o día máis feliz*, you brat, it's your First Communion. In the sky, all the angels are watching you, blond, dressed in white, flapping their little white-feathered wings, just so. What an outfit, how elegant you look in that sailor's suit, you look just like an admiral or elephant. The white shoes are a bit tight, they don't fit you very well, they belonged to your brothers. They hurt your feet, but you'll have to put up with them, crybaby, later, in the afternoon, you can take them off, you're hungry, well, you'll just have to lump it, you can't eat before taking Communion, it's a mortal sin, you're about to consume the Sacred Host for the first time in your life, Our Lord Jesus Christ is going to enter, to abide in your body, the Host is His Body, His Sacred Body, the bread transformed into the Flesh of Christ, and you're going to receive the Host, open your mouth, stick out your tongue, the priest will place the Host on your tongue, don't let it fall, put your tongue back in and swallow, just so, don't let it touch your teeth, if it touches your teeth, it's a mortal sin – no, venial – or was it mortal? – get out of the way, otherwise I'll thump you, all you do is get in the way, you dumb idiot. They're pretty, those white gloves, white hands, the missal with its gold corners and the figure of Christ etched on the white plastic cover, today He will enter inside you, you'll have Him inside you, and you must make sure you don't sin, you don't disappoint Him, though then there'll be a party, doughnuts in the sitting room, chocolate, sugared buns, will you get out of the way, you little midget? Take that. Now, don't start crying. You should have got out of the way when I told you, go and wash your face, go on, you can't receive First Communion with a tear-stained face. A tear-stained face. Tear-stained.

Sin City (Sacred History)

Men with small, dark eyes hold the book pressed against their chests and, with the other hand, cling to the handles of knives as they walk around the city's walls, muttering prayers and gazing at the victims of hunger and fear who stare down from on high, trusting only in the solid stone structure. They tear their clothes, roll around in the dust and smear ashes on their hair, honouring Yahweh God, who orders them to mow down the unrighteous like dried grass and to enlighten their enemies so the groans and laments will increase and praises be sung to Yahweh God.

They hold the book pressed against their chests because, in it, ancient prophets repeatedly affirm, when they ring out their trumpets made of the horns of oxen sacrificed in honour of the Most High, the foundations will tremble, the binding stones will crumble, and the walls of the impious Jericho will fall down with a great clamour and cloud of dust. They tear their clothes, roll around in the dust and smear ashes on their hair, honouring Yahweh God, who removes any obstacles so they can wield the knives the blacksmith has anointed in the blood of a castrated goat offered to Yahweh God so they won't fail when they wrest the voices from those throats that do not sing praises to His Name.

They hold the book pressed against their chests, having brought it with them from afar, the flocks of goats and sheep abandoned to the care of enslaved herdsmen, the fields of rye to the attention of women and the uncircumcised, for obedience guides them and, in the book, He has said, when they ring out their trumpets, the walls will fall down, and they will be able to put all the sinners of perfidious Jericho to the blade. They tear their clothes, roll around in the dust and smear ashes on their hair in honour of Yahweh God, who has ordered them not to leave a single man or woman, boy or girl, or animal, alive in the city so their blood will be spread over the paving stones of Jericho and praises be sung to His Glory.

No one will be left alive, as the book prescribes and foretells, except for a girl of no great age who will abandon the ruins, rubble and carrion to walk with miniature steps to other cities that do not sing praises to Yahweh God, but she won't be able to relate what is in her eyes because no words will emerge from her throat and the inhabitants of those cities won't know about the men heading towards them, bearing His Name and the book close to them.

It Was Not Me (Go On, Cry)

'Pardon me, don't hit me any more.

'Father, don't hit me. I said I was sorry.'

'Ah, now you're sorry? Go on, cry. Have you forgotten about your food? Have you forgotten?'

'I have.'

'Go on, then, cry. Now stand up. And remember next time.'

'Yes, father.'

'Are you sure you'll remember?'

'I'll remember.'

The Worshipful the Mayor of Vilanova

My name is María do Carmo Fernández Alvite and I am a teacher at Vilanova Primary School. I am writing to inform you about the situation of a pupil of mine, María Vanesa Gerpe Añón, aged five. She is the youngest daughter of a family made up of a father, mother and grandmother (she has other siblings, but they have been taken in by other families). The adults she lives with have shown repeated evidence of their inability to take charge of the girl's education and needs, an atmosphere at home that is revealed in the following aspects.

It is normal for her to present an extremely dirty, untidy and malodorous appearance. They do not wash her or give her clean clothes. This leads to a strong rejection among her classmates, who tend to marginalize and make fun of her.

The lack of attention and care she has suffered is so great that, on four occasions so far this year, she has come to school with soiled knickers. On one occasion, we gave her a bath at school and clean clothes; on another occasion, she came back in the afternoon in the same condition. This is due to the fact that most days she wakes up, gets dressed and comes to school all by herself, while the others are asleep, and sometimes there is nobody at home when she returns for lunch, forcing her to seek food from a neighbour.

She is used by her mother and grandmother to go begging in Vilanova and the surroundings. This, and the family's lack of care, have often led to her missing half a day's school, against her will, which is that of a child who has escaped just so she can attend classes. She is also often unpunctual.

She frequently looks tired on account of the exploitation she suffers, the malnourishment and the fact she doesn't get regular hours of sleep (she has been seen with her father in bars late at night). Her height and weight are among the lowest in her group. She often complains of stomach cramps.

Overall, she is a vivid, intelligent and hard-working child with a keen interest in learning and attending school. She is, however, confronted by a series of problems that have to do with the atmosphere at home. Fundamentally, deficiencies in language (problems of auditory and phonetic discrimination, incorrect sentence construction, and so on), in psychomotor development (slow movement, lack of energy...), she has problems socializing and is highly immature in certain aspects, lagging behind those of a similar age, as well as showing insufficient cultural knowledge. She uses lies as a means of defence and to get what she wants. It is also normal for her to commit petty thefts in class and to hog all the didactic materials for herself.

That said, she offers a very positive response when treated with affection and sympathy.

For all the above reasons, I judge it necessary, on account of the girl's physical and mental health, to find her another family to live with, where she can receive all the care and attention she deserves, since it is only in a loving and understanding atmosphere that a solution can be found to her problems. Problems that may not seem so important today, but that could have serious repercussions in the future in terms of learning, academic and even social integration.

I would like, therefore, to request that the councillor responsible for social welfare look into her case as a matter of urgency, given the girl's age and characteristics, and do everything possible to help her.

(From the Register)

Pretty Boy

'Pretty boy, pretty boy.'

'Pretty boy.'

'Go on, then, say "nice mamma". "Nice mamma".'

'Pretty boy.'

'No, no, no. Say "nice mamma". "Nice mamma".'

'Pretty boy.' The child laughs and shakes his blond, curly locks.

'All right then, well, I don't love you.' She takes him off her lap with a sour expression and plumps him down on the parquet floor. 'Mamma doesn't love you any more. Go and find somebody else to love you.'

The child turns serious, his mouth wide open, and stares at his mother sitting on a chair silhouetted against the window of a grey day. He contorts his features, goes red and bursts into tears.

His mother picks him up and starts to cuddle him.

'Poor little baby. It's nothing, my love. It's all over. My darling love. Here you go, have a sweet. Pretty boy.'

The Child and the Sea

The ambulance is silent, but the red light keeps turning round and round, as if emitting a long, piercing howl. The seagulls continue to fly, but nobody pays them any attention. The Red Cross volunteers push a gurney with a small shape draped in a white sheet. Men, women and lots of children crowd around the ambulance with grave expressions. A little apart from the others, two girls sit crying on a stack of fish crates. The day is still sunny, but a cold wind sweeps across the wharf. Nobody's bothered about the wind, they're all staring at the ambulance in silence.

The teacher talks anxiously to the Red Cross volunteers.

'I can't go with you. If I could, I'd accompany the boy, but I have to stay here with the others,' he points at the silent, frightened-looking children.

Bird comes up with a plastic bag on which is written 'Paqui Shoes, Becerreá' and places it by the gurney in the ambulance.

One of the volunteers takes the plastic bag and gives it back to the boy.

'You keep it, he's not going to need it any more.'

'It's his lunch,' the teacher remarks to the volunteer.

One of the ambulance men then slams a door, a little arm falls off one side of the stretcher, revealing the sleeve of a wet, green jersey and a little hand. He closes the other door and jumps into the passenger seat.

The ambulance starts wailing, the children and people move aside. It pulls off, climbing the slope that leads from the wharf to the houses. Everybody looks in that direction. Bird, his eyes wide open, nibbles on a chorizo sandwich he has taken out of the plastic bag.

'Ah, Bird, for goodness' sake,' says the teacher, 'couldn't you keep an eye on your little friend? You're always together, and yet today... just when I let one of you out of my sight.'

'I stopped with the others to watch a lady sewing.'

'What are you doing, you wretch? Eating the dead boy's sandwich? You wretch. Take that, and that!'

A woman protects the boy and hugs him close, turning her back on the teacher.

'Don't hit the poor thing, don't hit him. Calm yourself, don't hit him. It's enough tragedy for one day. The poor child has gone now.'

The teacher produces a handkerchief and uses it to wipe his face and rub his eyes. Bird pulls away from the woman and grabs hold of the teacher's jacket.

'He wanted to see the sea!' he exclaims in a rage.

The teacher places a hand on the head of the boy weeping next to him and stares out to sea.

'What a terrible tragedy! What made me think of bringing you to see the sea? We were all so looking forward to it.'

The children huddle around the teacher and the boy. Little Vanesa comes over to see Bird crying, contorts her face and starts crying softly as well.

'Don't take it so badly, little children, your friend is in heaven now,' says one of the women, in tears. 'There, the Almighty will be waiting for him.'

What?

'What?'

'I don't know.'

'What?'

'I don't know. I don't understand about such things.'

'What?'

'What do you want me to say? I told you I don't understand about such things, it's not my field. Had you asked me about the way to milk a goat, the molecular structure of tungsten, the importance of chamber music in the collected works of Brahms, love as a perversion of desire, the alterations caused by the use of chemical fertilizers in acidic soil, how to remove an ink stain from a cotton shirt, a reader's sickly voyeurism, the erosive effect of wind and water on granite rock, of time on neurotics, order and chaos, structure and absence in literary works, how to push a handcart with a minimum amount of effort...'

(From Nano's notebook *Philosophies*)

Getting Up Early

How sleepy she felt! Light filtered in around the edges of the blinds. Lace curtains. She had just woken up. She covered her face – how cold it was outside – and curled up into a ball. Her feet came into contact with a shape, a pair of legs. There was somebody else in the bed, someone with her in that bed. She moved her feet away slowly, carefully. Remained motionless. Where was she? She had just woken up, so she had slept there that night. Now the light of morning was filtering in. Who was at her side? She lay still. She had to get out of there. First of all, she removed her feet, slowly, without making a noise, making sure not to ruffle the sheets, then she slipped out her whole body. There were some red slippers on a flowery carpet, she put them on. She could feel her large, drooping breasts under her nightshirt. On the bedside table, there was an alarm clock, a crossword magazine and what looked like an oil lamp. She turned around and stared at the shape in the bed. It was a man. Balding. And fat. A large, hairy hand stuck out. She looked for the door, it was on the other side of the bedroom. She passed in front of a wardrobe mirror, glimpsed her own image, fat, peroxide blonde, came back and stood there for a while. How old was she? Fifty something. Fifty-seven or fifty-eight. She had wrinkles under her eyes and at the corners of her mouth. Reflected behind her was the form of the man in the bed. She left without making a noise and carefully pushed the door to.

A dark corridor, there was an open door out of which emerged the greyness of dawn. She walked slowly. It was a kitchen. Through a window with semi-transparent, plastic curtains filtered the light from a light well. The kitchen was small. So was the bedroom, the whole flat must be pretty small. This must be her home. She was the housewife. And that fat man was her husband. Did he love her? Who knows? Perhaps they had children. She switched on the light. There was a small fridge on the right. She opened it. A couple of chicken legs on a plate. Tomatoes, vegetables, a milk jug. Breakfast. She really should prepare breakfast. Where was the coffee? Or did they drink hot chocolate? That alarm clock would go off soon. What time was it set for? She closed the fridge without making a noise, crept towards the bedroom, went in, the fat man was still asleep. She went over to the bedside table, grabbed the alarm clock and held it in the light filtering through the blinds. It was a few minutes to eight, and the clock was set for eight. She quietly put the clock down and stole out of the room. She went back to the kitchen. Where were the matches?

Mother

I have just woken up in the early morning on account of the dampness I can feel on my legs. I have just woken up and my eyes are wide open because I know I've done it, I've gone and done it again. I knew this would happen. I don't want to wet myself, I always make sure I do a wee and empty my bladder before going to bed so I won't have to get up in the night or wet myself. But it doesn't work, I wet myself all the same. My eyes are wide open because I can feel the dampness and don't know what to do. Had I woken up when I started doing a wee, perhaps I would have had time, I could have squeezed my willy and dashed to the toilet. But I always wake up after I've done it. Now I'm afraid, that's why I stay still and my eyes are wide open, I'm afraid mother will find out. She's already warned me. 'I've told you a hundred times, you're too old to be wetting your bed.' It can't be true, but she said it very seriously. She would cut it off. It can't be true, but that's why I am afraid, my eyes are wide open, and I keep hold of my moist willy. She said it very seriously. Perhaps, instead of cutting it off herself, she'll call the castrator or have a word with Uncle Adolfo, who's a butcher and has very large knives. Whenever I wake up, I'm always cold in the night, perhaps that's why I wet myself. How unlucky, mother insults me and laughs at me. I stay still, my eyes wide open, thinking of sad things, because I am sad, I feel like crying, and also I am afraid. I can see a little light now, someone has switched on the light on the landing. I turn around slowly, there's a glow under the door. Now it opens, and I can see mother's figure coming towards me. She's smiling. Now she slips her hand into the pocket of her dressing gown and pulls out some large scissors that go 'snip, snip'. She smiles and says, 'Didn't I warn you?' Snip, snip. How unlucky.

Driver

Crossing waking or sleeping cities, *cidades malas*, sometimes by day, others by night, *todo o día e toda a noite*, running down roads full of sun and vehicles, *correr, sempre correr*, passing by people, *demasiada xente*, more people, but no, there's no rest *aquí* or *acolá*, *en todas partes* or *en calquera parte*, because you're a strange bird, *paxaro negro*, you don't find, you only seek, what the hell are you looking for, *que* the hell *buscas*, your eyes wide and nobody, *ningunha persoa*, you want somebody to write to you, you have no time to stop and I'm the one scripting the film.

Second Sorrowful Mystery

MEMORY AND DREAM

What about Peter Pan, then? A good beating. That's what I'd give that little twerp. What on earth is he about? What does that moron want? What's that prick up to? Is he dumb or eating shit? Damn monkey. I can't bear the guy, I don't want him in front of me. Listen, that guy really gets on my tits. Were it up to me, I'd send him off on a boat to the Gran Sol for the rest of his days. Come on, tell me, how can anyone want to remain a child for all eternity? Let someone come and explain it to me, and I'll smash his face in. I'm not generally violent, but there are some things... Listen, were I in charge, I mean really in charge. Not in the world, in life. Were I in charge of life, the first thing I'd do is ban childhood. Right away. Then I'd abolish adolescence as well, the way Abraham Lincoln did with slavery. That's an American president with a hat and beard, who got shot, the way happens in America. Adolescence is when you're not a child any more, but you haven't become an adulterer yet. That would get rid of lots of the suffering that's out there. All those murderers and psychopaths running around loose, I bet it all came from some trauma they suffered. If you undergo a trauma, it always repeats, right? Positively, a trauma is bad news. As is frustration. Frustration is also pretty bad. It all depends on how great the frustration is, but it's also pretty bad. If you put a trauma and frustration together, if you combine the two, well, that's the worst there is. People's childhoods are full of traumas and frustrations. You better believe it, I was a child for many years. Besides, I think about these things a lot, I spend the whole day turning them over in my mind, it's like with pencils and sharpeners, the more you turn them over, the sharper they become. And I am always thinking about children. Because I'm always thinking about life, eh. If you think about life, if you think deep down, right down to the bottom, so to speak, if you give it plenty of time and follow the path in front of you, well, you get to some conclusions. But to reach conclusions you have to go down to the base, the root of things, grab them where it hurts, which means going back to childhood. You have to go back to the children we were back then, that's, well, very, very important. Check out the children, and then ask what about that child, where is that child now?... Investigate what happened to him. Or her, supposing it's a girl, women make up more than half of the world, without counting the Chinese. You have to investigate because, if there was a boy or a girl, and they're not around any more, that means the boy or girl has died. Do you follow me? And if they've died, well, what did they die of? Or, to put it another way, who killed them? These things have to be looked into because, if you don't know about these things, then what the hell do you know about? Investigating is important, especially when we're talking about a crime, murder, and not illness. The saddest thing is when you start investigating and find out you were the guilty party. You killed the child that was and is no longer. Ooh, that's the worst-case scenario. That's a heavy-duty trauma and frustration. Positively. Because there's no healing that crime. Supplanting the child that was, well, we all do that, more or less, I've weighed up that question. But supplanting the child by means of murder, ooh, that's a major crime. It can't be healed. Whoever did that will have to carry the body of that boy or girl for all eternity, eternal punishment. I wouldn't want that. Childhood is a really fucked-up life, the child always ends up dying. Childhood should be banned, that's what I say, you may think me dumb, but I assure you I'm not. I may be lacking in certain areas, I'm even going a bit bald. The years pass, they pass so much it's frightening. I used to have a lot more hair, I used some product that is supposed to stop your hair falling out, but not a bit of it. I can still remember when I used to go about in a pair of shorts, now I can feel myself shrinking and losing my hair. The years attack you from behind. You don't realize it's happening, you're thinking about something else, working and so on. Or like me, thinking about things, turning them over in your mind. And in the meantime, the years, they weigh down on you, wear everything out, shrivel your joints and bones. They're probably the ones that kill children. I bet you that's right. Time is the Bogeyman's biggest trap. Or perhaps they're one and the same. Whatever, I tell you the saddest thing is when children die early. Before their time has come. Before the years get them. I mean those who die of an illness, or starvation, or because they've been run over. Or murdered. That's the saddest thing there is. It's so sad it wrings my heart and causes me pain. Like it was breaking. I don't even want to think about the pain involved, it makes me suffer. Don't even ask me about it. I often ask myself where do those children who die end up? I suppose they end up in the Land of Dead Children. I don't think they're with the other souls. I reckon they go to their own special place. And when I fall to thinking about the Land of Dead Children, I feel a particular pain. It must be pretty cold in that place. It's better not to think about it, because if you think about it... Better not to. Sometimes, at night, I dream. You dream even if you don't want to, that's the bad thing about it, your head does things without asking your permission. I dream I'm off to the Land of Dead Children. I'm walking along a narrow, tarmacked road and, standing on either side, there are dead children, their eyes wide open, staring at me, watching me pass. Others are walking alongside, across patches of mud and fields, but as soon as they catch sight of me, they gaze at me with those wide open eyes. I'm afraid, you bet I am, they're so stricken with cold I know if they could, they would kill me so they could open me up and retrieve the heat from inside me. I feel sorry for them, but I'm also afraid. I carry on, keep going, to see if there's a way out of that country. And when I wake up from that dream, you can't imagine how I breathe. Other times, I dream of a house in the middle of a forest, it has a gallery, out of which peep the little faces of children stricken with fear and cold. I am afraid. I have the impression in the end we're all going to be fodder for the Bogeyman. When we die, I think our punishment is going to be watching how he opens us up and pulls out the corpse of the child we used to be and carry inside us, and then devours it. The suffering will be terrible, the sense your heart is being consumed. I've dreamed that and I think it's true, but what's the point of talking about it, all anyone's going to do is laugh at me. I love children a lot, but I'm also afraid of them. I suppose I can see they're condemned to die. One way or another. Life's a fucking mess. I wouldn't mind meeting God one day, so I could give him a good hiding. I mean, a really good hiding. I suppose it's because I think a lot. That's my misfortune, thinking too much. There are some who just float through life. I don't know if they're dumb or what. Probably what. I think they just pretend to be dumb, as if they haven't cottoned on to what a fucking mess life is. Like my aunt Socorro. She married my uncle Manolo, who was somewhat lacking in initiative. They had children and all that, their children got married, and then my uncle passed away. They were a very formal couple, neither she nor my uncle ever made off with anybody else, my uncle was particularly lacking in initiative. What he liked was working, he seemed almost Catalan, they're supposed to like business more than women. But my uncle didn't have a mindset for business, he just kept on working like a packhorse. In that sense, he was very Galician. The point is my uncle Manolo died, and my aunt, in less than a year, well, she got hooked up with a friend of my uncle's who's married. Is that normal for a woman who never did anything out of the ordinary in thirty-five years of marriage? Is that normal? I'm not judging her for making off with someone else. We're all adulterous people, we know what we're doing, my uncle has left, it doesn't hurt him, and at least she gets to slake her thirst, everybody has to have something. Even so, if a woman who's almost in her sixties hooks up with someone else less than a year after she's been widowed, how is it she never hooked up with someone before? Because I have it on good authority that never happened. This woman – my uncle Manolo was so lacking in initiative, I'm sure he never made a move, all he could think about was work – this woman, if she put up with it for so long, it's because she was an artist. Going off to Mass, novenas, sundry anniversaries, and what have you. All those things. And as soon as she got the itch, nothing. She must have been play-acting all the time. This woman is an artist, a real actress. Ever since my brother-in-law Paco told me she's been having an affair, well, I've felt more respect for her. She seemed like a nun, with some people there's no telling. Though I have to say the women in this country are pretty amazing. Women here are something else. Positively. That's been scientifically proven. But the rain won't stop. How I wish I was in the Amazon. Or in the southern seas. Travelling on a ship across the southern seas. Crossing the ocean. Knowing you've a love who's waiting for you in port. Your own house. That's a nice idea. Like that Odysseus, the Greek king who went through hell and high water just to get home. That's a proper adventure. You never know, you might be travelling on a ship, calculating how you're going to return, when suddenly bish-bash! Time never passes in vain. Time kills everything. Kills us all. Rather than boarding a ship with plans to return, it would be better to hop into a car and leave for ever. Never stop, just keep on travelling. Never stop to talk to anybody, crossing countries where you know you're a stranger, an outsider, nobody knows you. Carry on like that. Vanish into the world. As if you've died. There was a film about some guy who kept driving his car. Thing is, I don't like travelling, and that's why I stay put. Besides, I don't have a licence. But sometimes I wish I could. I'd put on a pair of dark glasses, so nobody could see my eyes, so nobody could know me, and I'd drive and drive. For years on end. For ever. You just have to be careful you don't run over any children or dogs, they're always jumping out into the road.

Again

Again. Not again. This was the third time in five days it had happened to him, that he'd come out of the lift and found a different hallway. This one was dark, the typical carpet stretching from the entrance of the lift down two steps to the front door. The typical flowerpot with plastic plants in it over on one side. He looked at the mailboxes. There was a box with his name, that wasn't his box. See if there's any correspondence. No, nothing. God dammit, he banged it with his hand. It was enough to drive you mad. The hallway of your block keeps changing, some builders should be shot.

He traipsed over the carpet. He opened the door and emerged into the street. The terrible thing was until now he'd always found it changed as he was leaving his apartment, but any day now it could change when he was out, and then perhaps he wouldn't be able to locate his block. Would the front of the building change as well? And the number? He quickly turned around. 78. No, of course not, the number couldn't change, otherwise how would his mail arrive? That said, recently he hadn't been getting much mail. Who knows, perhaps the number had changed.

And what would the neighbours say about the changes? That was anyone's guess, you never got to meet the neighbours in that block, all you ever saw were new faces. Probably they rented an apartment for a season or a couple of months. They came and went, always new faces. Perhaps they hadn't even realized. Did he have his wallet? He fumbled in his jacket pocket. Yes. What a relief, if he got locked out, it was good to have his identity card at least. You never knew, it might never happen, but if it did, he didn't want to get stuck in the street without papers. Without ID, how could you prove you were who you said you were? Who would believe you if you didn't have your ID? He fondled the wallet in his jacket pocket, checked the time, quickened his pace, it was getting late.

Harmony (Abbreviated Long Novel)

Socorro met Manolo at a dance during Ascension. He wasn't from the area, he'd come with a group that included some locals: Moncho the pastry cook and one or two others. He asked her politely to dance – 'Would you care to dance?' he said – and then they talked as they were dancing, his name was Manolo, hers was Socorro. He was a little shorter than she was. She worked at a hairdresser's, 'Oh, you hairdressers are a conceited bunch,' he laughed. He danced very well and, when he laughed, he looked much better. He was missing a side tooth, which he later replaced with a gold one. The song soon finished, and they went their separate ways, each back to their own group. But the point was he asked her to dance again, and they carried on talking, he was clearly well-mannered and withdrawn, a little on the shy side. He informed her he worked in a bank, as an office boy. He was confident he would get promoted in a year's time, it was obviously true, and he seemed very formal. They arranged in another eight days to attend a dance at the Cine Radio, which had closed and was now a dancehall. That was how it all began. Things followed their course, and then they decided to get married. She left the hairdresser's, it had been a nice period when she was working, she and her work colleagues had got on like a house on fire. How they'd cried the day she stopped working! But such is the way of things, married people need a home of their own, and someone has to look after it. By now, Manolo had ascended to clerk, and he took on some accounts to do in the afternoon, so they had no problems renting a small apartment they found in Rosario.

At their wedding, needless to say, there were lots of people and plenty of fanfare. She felt very nervous that day. She'd always looked forward to getting married, but if there was something that put her off, it was the wedding night. She felt very nervous, even though she'd had a chat with Puri, who'd been married for two years. She'd never wanted to do it before, and now she felt a little afraid. Manolo had suggested doing it earlier, but she'd made it very clear he wasn't to try until they were married. In fact, it was nothing out of this world and didn't hurt that much. His thing was long and hard, she couldn't believe it could get like that, and he inserted it very slowly, he was very considerate. He obviously enjoyed it, he must have done it before, though she didn't ask, it hurt a little when he inserted it fully, but she didn't complain, the first few times you just have to put up with it. When he finished, he asked if she'd liked it, and she said she had. They chatted for a while about whether they'd prefer a boy or a girl, and then he suggested doing it again, and she said all right.

Soon after that, Manoliño arrived, and that was when they bought the apartment, which, although it had to be paid for – it took years and hard work – was well worth it, the flat had cost half a million, but now would fetch at least ten. What was more, there was a big difference between living where they had before to living in the centre, a big difference, it was like another life. Moving flat was the best thing they ever did, and it was all because she came up with the idea. Had it been up to Manolo, they would have stayed in Rosario, paying rent to old Matías. Oh no, Manolo had never been one for initiative or foresight; had it not been for her, she was always more ambitious... He had been more driven when he was single. That said, he'd always been a good husband, he hadn't been distracted by bars, gambling, women or anything like that. And in his role as a father, well, Manoliño and Anita could be happy he'd never lifted a hand against them. He'd always been affectionate, perhaps a little too good, a father sometimes needs to lay down the law or to give the children a smack. But he'd never been that impulsive, sometimes you should be, otherwise you can be made to look like an ass. Had it not been for her – she'd always stood behind him – he would never have got on in life. Afonso was a good friend, but had she not urged him on, Afonso would have grabbed his promotion, it was his turn, he'd been there longer, but had he stayed still, Afonso or somebody would have taken it, a bleating sheep loses a bite... Manolo was always like that, a little lacking in initiative. Afonso, well, he was different. Pereira as well. Afonso was clearly a lout, he can't have been a very good husband. But he was fun. One day, they'd all gone to the beach: Manolo, she, Afonso and Fina. The two couples had left the children with their grandparents and gone off in the white Fiat 600 they had back then. What fun they'd had that day, they'd eaten a potato salad she had made and a pie cooked by Fina. She'd worn her red bathing suit, it fitted her very well, she hadn't lost her figure, ever since Anita she'd had these large breasts, no man would ever walk past and not linger over them. Afonso, well, he'd had a good look, she'd felt a little embarrassed, not because of Manolo, who hadn't even noticed, but because of Fina, they were good friends. They'd all drunk and got very merry, Afonso had made out he was going to get on top of Fina, you could see it was hard under his trunks, it looked pretty large, Fina laughed and told him to stop mucking about, Afonso laughed back. What a brute! He certainly wasn't very educated. Or sensible. But they'd had fun that day. It had been a nice period, when the children were young. They used to leave them with their grandparents, and not a week went by they didn't go to the cinema a couple of times.

Then the children had grown up. Anita was on the verge of graduating. How old it made you feel. It seemed like Manoliño had just put on his first pair of trousers and already he had a girlfriend. How quickly the years went by; before you realized, a child was graduating and getting married. How quickly the years went by. Rosi was a good daughter-in-law, a little stuck-up, but all women are like that nowadays, they all have plenty of time to go to the hairdresser's, but sometimes leave the house in a mess. Not Rosi. She ran a tight ship. Then along came the children: first Patricia, followed by Rafael. How pretty they were! Patricia was just like her father when she was little; Rafael, on the other hand, inherited his mother's traits. You have children, and then there are grandchildren. Life is like that.

The one who failed to adapt was Manolo. Ever since he'd retired, he hadn't left the house, all day watching television. He'd never hung out in bars when he was young and now he spent the whole day cooped up at home. She kept telling him to pop down the bar or the pensioners' club for a while. 'Why don't you give Pereira a call and go to the football?' But no. Even if it was just to get him out of the way so she could clean the house, it was impossible. Sometimes the two of them would go out for a walk or to the cinema. Just so they could leave the house; she preferred watching films on television, in the cinema her feet got frozen. The other day, they'd bumped into Fina as she was coming back from six o'clock Mass. Poor woman. She must have been bored out of her mind since Afonso died. Poor fellow, he'd still been young when he passed away. In good shape, too. He'd died of lung cancer, he'd always been a heavy smoker. That was six or seven years ago. How quickly life went by! She couldn't complain. The children were grown up, Anita had got herself a public-sector job, and hers had always been a harmonious marriage.

Itchy Finger

There were clouds in the sky, dark ones, but there was also a little bit of light, which made it easier to travel. On clear days, he even enjoyed driving, up in the driver's seat, steering the coach, devouring the road.

He drove distractedly, picking his nose with the little finger that was missing the uppermost phalanx. The phalanx had been missing for years, but in the last few days he'd again felt some discomfort in his finger. It wasn't pain, it was just more sensitive. As if he'd lost the phalanx not long ago. He pulled it out, looked at it and rubbed it against his thumb, then changed gear.

To think, when he was a boy, he'd got carsick whenever he boarded a coach. The way things turn out. And now he'd just gone around all the bends from Muros to Noia, as every day, without even thinking about it. There used to be more curves, the road had improved a lot. He wished it had been like that when he'd started out in that old banger.

How many years had he been with Castromil? It would be thirty-two years in March. No, thirty-three. Thirty-three years in the same company. And forty spent driving. First lorries, then coaches. He'd got his licence when on military service, after that all he did was drive. They were passing A Barquiña at the entrance to Noia. 'Here we are, ladies and gentlemen!' Passengers started shuffling about in their seats. The avenue of trees was devoid of people owing to the morning cold. A woman with a grey coat and a green plastic bag stood waiting in the doorway of the

La Terraza café. When she saw the bus, she disappeared inside. To warn the others. He veered over to the right, alongside the pavement, and parked.

He opened the doors and switched off the engine. There was a silence he valued more highly every day.

'Here we are! Time for a coffee.'

Passengers stood up and started speaking in loud voices. He pulled out a cloth from under the radio and wiped the steering wheel. When he was young, and not so young, he'd enjoyed listening to the sound of the engine. Now he didn't even like the hum of a brand-new car. He was obviously getting old. He put the cloth back under the radio.

'We're early today!' said an old man in a raincoat who'd boarded in Esteiro and was now carefully descending the steps.

It was true, there was almost no traffic on a Monday morning. He got out of the driver's door. He found it difficult to move his legs after being seated for so long. He huddled up and vigorously rubbed his hands together to drive away the cold. His breath formed a cloud in front of him. He opened the boot on the side, and a young man in a sailor's uniform retrieved his kit bag.

'Hope you enjoy your leave.'

'I'll try to.'

He closed the boot and headed in the direction of the bar.

The barman, a frail man in his fifties with sideburns and slicked-back grey hair, was sweeping behind the counter. He propped the broom against the coffee machine and served the sailor a brandy. A woman in mourning and a girl sat at a table. The driver went over to the counter.

The barman brought him a coffee, in which he sprinkled a few drops of brandy. The driver deposited a few coins next to the cup, and the barman picked them up.

'What's up, Antonio? You seem distracted, you haven't said a word.'

The driver attempted to smile.

'Nothing, I was just thinking.'

'Ah, thinking, I get it.'

The barman looked over at the seated woman and, from behind the counter, asked:

'What's it to be?'

'A white coffee and a small glass of warm milk.'

The barman started preparing them at the coffee machine.

'You know what I was thinking?' said the driver to the barman, who was gesturing in front of the machine.

'Could be anything. I sometimes think. And all sorts of things come up...'

'I was thinking how long I've been driving a coach.'

The barman placed the coffee and glass of milk on the counter, came out, passed behind the driver, who was blowing on his coffee, and picked up the smoking beverages. He carried them slowly towards the table where the woman and girl were sitting.

'Listen, it's for the girl. Don't you have a smaller glass? I did say a small glass.' The girl gazed at them both in turn.

The driver drank the rest of his coffee and pulled a silver biro and notebook out of his jacket pocket. With a concentrated expression, he flicked through the pages that had been written on and started jotting something down.

The barman went back behind the counter.

'Ten thousand,' said the driver with a sigh.

'Ten thousand what?' asked the barman.

'Ten thousand journeys. I have just multiplied the thirty-three years I've been working for the company by the number of trips each year. That's ten thousand, give or take. Ten thousand journeys.'

'Blimey.' The barman stood watching him, leaning on the handle of his broom. 'Ten thousand journeys. That's enough to get you to Australia. Thirty-three years...'

'That was Christ's age.' The driver slaps the counter. 'Better be off.'

'You really have travelled a lot. Thirty-three years...' mused the barman.

'Shame they're not millions...' remarked the driver as he went through the door.

'Time to go!' He jumped into his seat and made himself comfortable. There weren't many passengers today, the coach was almost empty. Strange for a Monday first thing. The sky had gone back to being ashen; if it didn't rain along the road, it would be raining in Santiago.

The woman in mourning and the girl sat down in the front seats, next to the door.

'Fasten your seatbelts and get ready for take-off. Destination Santiago,' said the driver in a low voice as he winked at the girl.

He started the engine and pressed down on the accelerator.

'Wait just a moment, there's a young man coming,' said the voice of a man from behind. A shiver ran down his spine, he didn't move. That voice had belonged to his father. It couldn't be, his father had died many years ago. It had sounded like him, but no. It must have been some other old fellow.

A slim young man with a trimmed moustache and cropped hair quickly boarded the bus. The driver recognized him at once, with absolute certainty. It was him when he was twenty or twenty-something. The young man showed him the ticket in his right hand, which had a bandaged little finger. The driver was dumbstruck, he couldn't speak, gazing at this young man with a boy's face who didn't know what to do with his moustache. Gazing at this young man standing there, showing him a piece of paper, in that chestnut-brown jacket he'd bought at the market, which had lasted until he got married at thirty-two, and those black trousers his mother had made for him. Loose-fitting, old-fashioned clothes. His own clothes. Himself.

'Please sit down,' he stammered finally. The young man who was himself at twenty passed down the bus and took a seat.

The driver knew very well which seat he had taken. Next to the old man who'd just been coughing, next to his father. That cough day and night, which echoed through the house and wouldn't let him sleep. Awake at night, listening to him cough and hawk. He recalled the journey to Santiago, his father had gone with him to the doctor's, he didn't want to lose the whole finger. He hadn't wanted his father to go with him, he'd done his military service and knew how to handle himself on a visit to the doctor's to have his finger checked out. But his father had insisted on travelling with him. In their house, he was the one in charge. He was in charge, and nobody else. He again heard the familiar smoker's cough coming from behind.

'That's everybody,' said the woman travelling with the girl.

'Right you are,' the driver reacted slowly, 'let's go then.' He set the coach in motion. He stared in the rear-view mirror, searching among the vacant seats, and caught sight of that black hat his father used to wear when travelling from Noia to Santiago. He knew perfectly well who he would see if he got up and headed in that direction. His father sat, wearing his hat, rigid as a post. And in the other seat he could see his own forehead, not as broad as now and less wrinkled, the black hair all slicked back. A hand with a bandaged finger appeared in the hair. The driver passed his own hand over his head and then looked at the little finger that was missing the uppermost phalanx. He put the coach into reverse.

'Hey, hey! Stop, stop!' shouted people from behind. 'Where do you think you're going? You just hit a parked motorbike!'

He looked in the wing mirror and saw a motorbike lying on the ground. A young man came out of the bar and bent over to pick it up. The driver didn't wait and accelerated away. He finally reached the road that passed through the town and gradually left the houses behind. He felt dizzy, he couldn't hear the voices of the passengers on the coach discussing what had happened with the motorbike, all he could hear was the engine inside his own head. A furious engine that churned his senses.

What Did I Tell You?

What did I tell you, Irene? What did I tell you? Didn't I tell you you were going to stain your dress? Didn't I tell you? Didn't I tell you if you wore it today, you'd get it all dirty? Well, prepare yourself for when we get home, you're going to get a hiding. I'm going to warm the seat of your pants. You dratted nuisance, that's enough of that. What did I tell you, eh, what did I tell you? All you do, the two of you, is give me more work. What do you think, that you're going to get the better of me? Well, you couldn't be more mistaken, little missy. You're very wrong if you think you can do whatever you feel like, you and your father seem to want to ruin my health. What did I tell you, eh, what did I tell you? I've had it up to here with you. Sit quietly beside me. I warn you, if you move... On the new dress! See what you've gone and done, you look like you've just had a mud-bath. What did I tell you, eh, what did I tell you? I made it look so pretty, and now see what you've done. You're a mess. Damn child. Spoiled brat.

Disappear (from Sight)

The fog advances down the road, some twenty yards in front of the car. It approaches on either side, almost to the verge, revealing the hazy outline of the first trees that supposedly form part of the landscape, inside the fog. Pull over, switch off the engine. Leave the car in gear, put on the handbrake and get out of the car. Lock it. (Then throw the keys far away into the fog.) Start walking over the grass, the stones and ferns towards that damp, soft nothingness. Carry on walking, fewer brambles, less broom, stroking us as we pass. We carry on walking, further inside, and now we can't see anything in front of us, we can only feel scratches on our clothes, and we carry on walking and disappear into the fog, we carry on walking and carry on walking until we disappear. Disappear for good. We may end up in the Land of Dead Children. You never know.

(From the manual *Exercises in Self-Harm* by various authors)

Better Not to Talk about Such Things

He drove automatically. By the petrol station on the outskirts of town, he passed the bus coming from Santiago, the driver tooted and waved, but he didn't greet him. He didn't see him. His mind was full of images, he could barely see the road in front.

Images of his mother gliding silently around the house. Always doing something, permanently busy, but never opening her mouth. Like a soul in torment. Sometimes, when his father wasn't there, she would talk to him and ask, 'What does your schoolteacher have to say, Toniño? Is everything OK?' 'Everything's fine,' he would reply. 'Make sure you study, don't be lazy. When you get back from military service, I'll help you set yourself up in whatever you like. If you want to work the land, that's fine, something else, that's fine too. You hear me, Toniño?' 'I hear you.' 'Then talk, God dammit! Or don't you have a tongue? Make sure you study.' She asked him whether he had a tongue – she who spent whole days not opening her mouth, like a soul in torment.

There were times she talked in front of his father, those times she drank. He'd seen her on a few occasions, talking in a loud voice and asking him questions. 'When are you going to plough the Field in the Middle? Aren't you ever going to fix the leg of that bench?' Once, she had even been disrespectful. 'Hey, fly-by-night, aren't you ever going to retile the roof? Are you waiting for it to rain while you scratch your belly?' At this, his father had stood up without saying a word, grabbed his cap from a nail by the door and gone out into the night. When the two of them were left alone, she had fallen quiet.

Sometimes, when he was a boy and the two of them were going to work in a field or to mow the grass, she would tell him stories and make him laugh with remarks about the neighbours. Those days were like a party to him.

He again heard the old man's cough. He looked in the rear-view mirror and could see the black hat and the slicked-back hair. One next to the other, without moving. His father, on the other hand, had always talked to him. He was always asking him questions – not about school – and telling him to do things. The point was he talked to him. He explained how to do things, how to use sulphate, how to remove potato eyes, how to load the cart properly... He was always talking to him, teaching him things. He climbed the curves and slopes of San Xusto, the engine roared, he changed gear and switched on the windscreen wipers. The windscreen cleared, and he could see the new roof of the old church down in the valley, in amongst the trees. He must be going crazy. If a man is confronted by his own dead father and himself when he's twenty-something, it's because he's gone crazy. They hadn't even said hello. No, they were like two strangers, sitting in the back. But if they did speak to him, what was he going to say? My goodness, he hoped they wouldn't. It was all because of the years. A man starts going crazy, but if he keeps quiet, the others may not notice. He wouldn't say a word. He would be as silent as the grave.

'It hasn't rained for a while,' remarked the woman travelling with the girl.

He heard her and mumbled something in reply. The finger would heal nicely, the doctor would say, he had to keep it bandaged and smear it with ointment. The truth was it had healed well. He couldn't even remember what his finger had been like before it lost the phalanx. Like the one on his other hand, he supposed.

'Are you feeling carsick?' he heard the woman asking the girl. The girl said something in a low voice.

'If the girl is feeling carsick, I have some sweets here,' offered the driver. He opened a little drawer under the counter for coins and pulled out three sweets. He stretched his hand outwards and backwards. The woman took the sweets.

'Thank you very much. Here you go, Yasmina, suck on these. See what a nice driver.'

It was better to spend a few pesetas on sweets than to have someone vomit on the coach. Hopefully she'd soon feel better. He looked in the mirror. There were the two heads, neither moving nor talking. They hadn't talked all day. He had blamed his father for the damage to his finger. They'd had an argument, he'd gone out into the yard and angrily started chopping wood. He'd cut off the end of his little finger and left it on the stump. He'd stopped talking to him, stopped answering his questions. But it wasn't like that, nobody had told him to go outside and chop wood after their argument.

A woman was waiting with an open umbrella at the stop in Urdilde. He slowed down, parked and opened the door. The woman closed her umbrella.

'Good day to you,' said the woman as she got on. She held out a hand with some coins, and the driver took them. The woman sat down behind the lady in mourning and the girl.

The old man carried on coughing, it was a bad cough. He knew all about that. He closed the door and pulled away.

The mist had turned into a light drizzle, which the windscreen wipers cleaned off. It was a sad, hypnotic movement that kept on repeating. They'd argued because his father had wanted him to stay at home. He had learned to drive lorries during his military service and wanted to work in that. He liked farming, but he wanted to work for himself, he didn't want to be at his father's beck and call all day long. Things always had to be the way his father decided. This had to be done like that, it always had been and always would be. 'When I die, you can do things your own way.' The old man's cough started up again. This time, it sounded stronger, further down, one was followed by another and, when it seemed all the air had run out, by another.

'Goodness, what a bad cough that gentleman has!' said the woman with the girl.

The driver looked in the rear-view mirror and saw that hat leaning forwards and shaking. Next to it, the motionless, combed hair, not moving towards the old man. He heard a car horn and turned the steering wheel, the coach swerved violently to one side. He'd almost collided with a car coming the other way.

'Hey, what was that?' asked the voice of a man from behind.

'The coach skidded, it's all this drizzle,' said another male voice.

'Crikey, we almost overturned,' remarked the woman who'd boarded in Urdilde.

He drove, clinging to the steering wheel. What a fright! He'd almost caused an accident. That cough needed curing. But no, that day they'd go to the doctor's, he wouldn't say a word to his father or answer his questions, they'd look at his finger, but keep quiet about the cough. He was always coughing, and it was getting worse. They'd get back home in the evening, and his father would go to bed. In the night, he would pass away.

He took an ironed, folded handkerchief out of his back pocket and wiped his nose. They were coming into Santiago, there were the usual cars for a rainy day. They stopped to queue at a traffic light.

'Could you open here and let us out?' asked the woman with the girl.

He pressed the button for opening the doors. But he didn't want the others to leave, he had to say something first. A few people leaped out of their seats and started exiting through the front and back doors. The old man and the young man as well, in silence. He had to talk to him, he was going to die the next day, lay aside their differences, he only had one day left, and it was better to die in peace.

The woman, holding the girl's hand, stopped in front of him and said:

'Thank you very much for the sweets. She's always getting carsick, but the sweets took her mind off it.'

'I'm glad, madam, please go quickly, the lights are about to change,' he said, scanning the people who had already got off and were walking along the pavement.

'Thank the gentleman, María Yasmina. Say thank you.'

'Please hurry, madam, the lights have changed. And tell that gentleman in the hat, walking with the young man, to have his cough checked out at the doctor's.'

'Which gentleman?' the woman gazed perplexedly in the direction he was pointing. 'Where?' The cars behind started honking their horns.

'That one. The one who's about to turn the corner, the one in a suit and hat. Please hurry.'

The woman pushed the girl slowly down the steps, and then descended herself. The horns grew louder. When he closed the door, the woman gave him a quizzical stare.

He pulled away, and the almost empty bus advanced silently towards the cars waiting at a light further on. His father wasn't going to have his cough checked out, and that night he'd cough and cough until he ran out of air. By the time his mother called him and he rushed to the bedroom, the old man would be lying still. After that, nothing. They'd bury him, and he and his mother wouldn't talk. A few months later, he'd up and leave.

His finger kept bothering him. And things were going through his head it would be better not to tell anybody. The years must drive you crazy. Better not to talk about such things with anybody. If only he could put in for early retirement. The traffic was always bad on rainy days. He didn't like travelling in winter.

Memory

I don't recognize this face at all, I've never had one like this before. What was my face like yesterday? I had black glasses. And my hair was black, not fair like it is today, or curly. It was straight. Yesterday, my face was very different, thinner. And it had a larger nose. Look at these spots, I bet you I bleed when I shave. At least tomorrow I won't have them any more. What will my face be like tomorrow? I liked the one I had two days ago, the one with the green dreamy eyes, the way women like them. That woman in red who stared at me in the park, the thing she liked about me yesterday was my romantic look. If I went for a walk today in the same place, we might bump into each other again. But even if I dared to talk to her, would she see in this vulgar, spotty face the delicate features and seductive eyes of the man she met yesterday? Every day is the same. I'd like to have the same face all the time. Just one face, only for me. How happy it would make me feel to come across that face with the green eyes in the mirror one morning! They were green, but with a hint of brown. I'd go looking for the woman in red and say, 'Remember me?' And she'd reply, 'Have we been introduced?' And then she'd let me walk by her side. Damn it, this hair is tricky to manage.

One Spring Day a Sailor

It was the kind of spring day when boats dock, bringing merchandise from afar and sailors with unusual tales of extravagant peoples and stunning animals. From one of those boats that had just come back from a long journey, a sailor quickly descended the gangway. He marched along the wharf, his gait still influenced by the rocking of the waves. Under his tilted cap could be seen the odd lock of grey hair, the seagulls screeched, and the sailor smiled, the words of an old ballad flickering about his lips.

As he passed beside the sardine fishermen, he heard a voice calling out to him.

'Hey, Rubén!' A man in a black woollen hat and yellow waterproofs wandered over the deck towards the prow, gesturing towards him.

He recognized him, it was Valentín, an old friend. But he was changed, much older, as if he'd been through a whole life. He jumped on to dry land and approached, holding out his hand and, without even allowing him time to take it, gave him a big hug. The man Valentín had become embraced him, shaking him and calling him by name.

'Rubén, Rubén! So many years! I thought you were dead.'

'Hi, Valentín. How's it going? You look older.'

'I look older? What do you think you look like? You think, after all these years, we'd be the same?'

'All these years? Has it been so long?'

'Of course it has. You were a lad when you went to sea, what do you think you are now?'

The sailor fell quiet, not knowing what to say as he scrutinized the years on his friend's face. He then looked down at his own feet and carried on upwards, trying to see himself.

'Don't listen to me, Rubén! Don't get like that! You're still the same young lad.' His friend grabbed his hand in confusion and shook it. He let go, and they turned to face the sardine boat.

'So long on board. You don't notice the years going by... I hadn't thought...' But his friend was already on deck, heading towards the stern.

'Valentín, wait!' His friend stopped and turned to listen. 'What happened to the others: Roberto, Rafael, Ramiro?' he shouted.

'They died during the war!' his friend shouted back, cupping his hands. He headed in the other direction.

'What war?' But his friend had already joined the other sailors astern and wasn't listening.

He slung his kit bag over his back and felt it heavier. He'd put too much stuff inside. He left the harbour among unfamiliar faces and wandered up the first streets with a sense of surprise. There were new buildings he hadn't seen before, some of the façades were pockmarked with gunfire and shrapnel. He vaguely recalled what these strange streets had looked like before.

As he passed in front of a low house, he saw a woman ironing in front of an open window. It was Elisa, his sweetheart. The years had passed for her as well, he thought, she looked paler and thinner, but preserved the elegance that had made him fall in love with her. She was moving her lips, probably singing a sad song the way she used to, while ironing the clothes. He went over to the window.

'Elisa, my love!'

She lifted her eyes and gazed at him with a look of surprise and recognition. Then with a mournful expression. She approached the window as well and leaned on the sill.

'Elisa, my darling! I was so anxious to come back and see you again. You're in a different house now.'

'Rubén,' she murmured.

'I've got money, lots of money. We can open the hotel I talked about in my letters.'

'Rubén, you've lost weight. And your hair has gone grey, Rubén.'

'Come outside. Or open the door. Don't pay any attention to my grey hair, I can dye it. Elisa, my heart is brimming with kisses for you. And I brought you this gift.' He took a silken parcel out of his kit bag and handed it to her slowly.

'Go on, open it.'

'Ah, Rubén! You're as eager as a child, and I'm tired by now.'

'Go on, open it.'

'Rubén, it's late. You never wrote, I thought you were dead.'

'I wrote letters. I told you I was coming. Go on, open the present.'

'Rubén, your letters never arrived. I got married, this is my husband's house. He works in an office,' she said, holding the package.

He stood open-mouthed. She removed the silk and pulled out a gleaming bead necklace.

'It's beautiful, Rubén. I'm just sorry your letters never came. You were such a happy young man...'

'So long on board... You don't notice the years going by... I'm not sure...'

'Here, I have to give it back to you. Go now, Rubén, my sweet. My husband won't be long coming back from work. He's a good man, and I don't want to upset him. You shouldn't have stayed away so long.'

He put the silk and necklace in his jacket pocket and left, dragging his kit bag along behind him. He walked a little way and then looked back. The woman was shutting the window with a sad expression, she gave a little wave and then closed the window.

He staggered along the pavement, he wasn't used to walking on dry land and his luggage was heavy. People passing by did not recognize him, and he thought he'd spent too long away at sea. He hadn't noticed the years going by, there must have been more than he'd realized. Time was treacherous and gave no warning.

He walked until he came to his own district. Unfamiliar houses, shops and faces. Some houses were still the same, just a little older. He searched for his own with quickened pace.

It wasn't there. The place it had occupied was now an empty plot strewn with rubble, earth and old wood. On the side of the house next door, at the height of the first floor, were remnants of blue paint from what had once been his bedroom. There was still a paper bird that he'd cut out of a magazine and stuck to the wall with mashed potato. His house wasn't there, it had been demolished.

It was all he could do not to sit on his kit bag and pine away. He sat on the pavement and tried to identify some of the stones from his old house in all that rubble. He thought it was possible to feel the same sickness he'd suffered the first three days at sea on dry land as well.

An old woman in mourning stopped in front of him and examined his face, searching for someone in his features.

'Is that you?' She carried on contemplating his face.

He gave her a weary look.

'Is that Rubén, María's son?'

'It is. What happened to my mother?'

'You've come back. No one ever thought you'd come back, we all thought you'd drowned.'

'Well, I have come back. What happened to my mother?'

'She died a long time ago. Soon after you left. She couldn't get used to the lack of news. She withered away and died like a little bird.'

'She died...'

'Of course she did. Didn't you think the time would go by? You're talking like a foolish boy.'

'And there was me, holding out hope all these years.'

'You should never have left, Rubén.'

'So long on board... You don't notice the years going by... I couldn't say...'

'You should never have come back, Rubén.'

'I should never have come back.' He struggled to his

feet and picked up his kit bag. Under its weight, he made as if to leave that district.

He caught a red tram with a large advertisement for 'Ithaca Sardines' on its side, which took him to the harbour. He was preoccupied and keen to abandon this city he didn't recognize. He watched as he passed in front of the house of his beloved. He thought he saw, behind the curtain, a man and a woman sitting on either side of a table, a soup tureen between them. But it may just have been his imagination.

He got off in the harbour and staggered along, the sardine boats had put to sea. The wharf was quieter now it was evening. He searched for his boat, but it wasn't there.

He asked a man in a blue apron, who was pushing a wheelbarrow laden with sacks.

'It weighed anchor half an hour ago.' He carried on exerting himself.

Standing there, the sailor felt infinitely tired and thought he should never have come back, he should never have got off the boat.

'I'm shipwrecked.'

The man pushing the wheelbarrow stopped and asked, 'What?'

But he didn't reply. He stared at the sea with all its pathways. The man with the wheelbarrow continued pushing his load.

It's a Joke

'Now for some fun, eh, so no getting serious. Everyone is to laugh and have a good time, so here's something to make you laugh. No more serious faces. Off they go! I said no more serious faces.

'OK, there was once an Englishman, a Dutchman and a Galician.'

'It's not like that. It's like this: there was once an Englishman, a Frenchman and a Galician.'

'No, it isn't. The way I tell it, it's a Dutchman. There was once an Englishman, a Dutchman and a Galician. And one of them goes and says...'

'Oh, come off it, it's not like that!'

'Listen, clever clogs, who's telling the joke anyway, eh? I'm the one telling it, right? Got it? So, there was once an Englishman, a Dutchman – because I fucking well feel like it – and a Galician. Enough of that. And one of them goes and says, "Let's make a test to see who has the biggest head of all three of us!" So, the Englishman goes and takes out a piece of paper full of mathematical problems and says, "See this?" In a minute, he starts multiplying from memory, square roots and what have you, mathematical operations, until bam! He's solved the problems, and the others are standing open-mouthed. So, the Frenchman goes...'

'You see how it was a Frenchman, and not a Dutchman after all?'

'So what then? I got it wrong, what's the matter with that? So, the Dutchman goes and starts reciting all the capitals of the world by heart: "Paris, Rome, Tokyo, Pakistan, Caracas..." The other two are amazed. "London, Paris, Moscow..." And so on, for ten minutes.'

'I know this one.'

'What do you know? Let me finish telling the joke. So, the Galician goes and takes off his cap and starts scratching his head. The others ask, "What is it, Galician, you scratching your head to summon the ideas?" And he replies, "No, ho. I'm warning all the lice to get out of the way. See that enormous oak? Well, check this out." He breaks into a run, headbutts the oak and knocks it over. "So, who has the biggest head, then?" he says. And he wins the bet.'

'What bet? You never said anything about a bet.'

'There was a bet. Didn't I tell you? I'm the one telling the joke. It has another ending. When it's the Galician's turn, he headbutts the others and knocks them down dead. Then he says, "So, who has the biggest head?"'

'Boh, I don't think that's funny. I knew it anyway.'

(From the spiritual manual *Exercises in Self-Hatred* by A. TEIJEIRO GERPE)

The Passage of Time

He's got really fat, really ugly. It's amazing, he used to be so handsome, unbelievable, really. You remember how handsome he was? He had this gorgeous face, with those green eyes. Ah, yes, those green eyes. You felt like you were dying whenever you stared into those eyes. Had he spoken to me while looking at me with those green eyes, I think I'd have fallen over. Ha, ha, don't let Andrés know! Were Andrés to hear that, he'd kill me, ha, ha. He was really very handsome, and had this gorgeous figure. All rigid and tense. He was like a Hollywood actor. Besides, there weren't that many tall men back then, now it's normal, but back then... You looked at him and felt like gobbling him up, he was a real bonbon. So he got what he wanted. You remember that Laura woman married to a mining engineer or something like that? She was crazy about him. So he did what he wanted. With the others as well – what was the name of that dark-haired girl who later married a merchant seaman? No, Mónica or something like that. He didn't hang around. You can imagine. He did well – if the invitation was open... And you bet it was, my goodness, if he'd looked at me with those eyes... You felt like eating him up. You seen what a belly he has now? And that double chin, which makes his face look all round and chubby? My goodness, he really got ugly. His eyes, yes, those are the same, but he isn't. He looks a bit dumb now. Yes, there's something strange about his expression. He must be on treatment for his nerves, that's what it is. Yes. Medicine like that will finish anybody off.

It makes you gain a lot of weight, which you then can't get rid of. It may just be the years, he's hasn't taken care of himself, he's let himself go. Or he's lost interest in women and gradually gone off. You betcha, at least twenty. Well, maybe not so many. Do you think he got married? My goodness me, he's really gone and got very ugly.

It's Not Time for Palms to Give Off Their Scent

(Nubian slave woman with thick, dark hair, dressed in typical Brazilian fashion with polka-dotted clothes and a headscarf tied at the front. She has a cigarette in the corner of her mouth and is mopping the floor.)

It's certainly not time for the palms to be giving off their scent. But they are. Their aroma is so sweet you might think the dates are ripe already, but it's not time for them yet! You might think so. Things are not how they should be – today I heard a dog miaowing and a cat barking, and the weather, you can't tell whether it's getting better or worse, the sky is out of sorts, the stars are all over the place. I have the impression these people's gods are not best pleased, that god they're supposed to have isn't always in the best of moods. I know a Nubian slave woman shouldn't be expressing her thoughts, my mouth will not utter a word, but all I see are omens around me. And this blood.

(She squeezes out the mop.)

This blood my mop can't get rid of. This blood I try to scrub off, but the Vileda's no use, it's stained red, I keep rinsing it out, it just gets red again, but doesn't clean or remove any of the blood. This Jewish blood is hard to clean, it's a stubborn kind of blood, none of the men or women in my country have such thick, dark blood. It leaves a bitter smell in the air, it must be from a male or female body some god has touched with his hand, it doesn't seem entirely human. May all my gods and the Jewish gods keep me from such a person, it's not right for us humans to get mixed up with gods or prophets, it can't be good. There's that man crying out again.

(She squeezes out the mop.)

There's that man who's been imprisoned in the well crying out again. And my mop just won't get rid of the stains. His shouts sound more threatening than other days – it's obvious, what with him being a saint, he's also been affected by these bad omens. Really bad, I mean. This stain is like dried plastic paint and just won't budge, even though I keep mopping the floor, soaking the mop in this devilish blood. May my household gods protect me, it wasn't my intention to offend any god or demon in this country of Jews who butchered so much and did so much evil in my land, their gods and demons must be a ferocious lot. May my household gods protect me from evil spells, I never meant to insult any god or demon in this land of my masters. There he goes again.

(She squeezes out the mop.)

There he goes again, crying out all the time, though his tone today is different, it's like he's calling to death – that's what it seems like to this poor, stupid Chaldean slave woman who doesn't understand the tongues of this country of grim-eyed men. It's better for a poor slave woman not to hear what her masters are talking about, in case she should discover secrets she's not meant to know and risk a hiding or a beating. He doesn't stop shouting, it sends a shiver down the spine of one who doesn't understand his speech and, unless he shuts up, he's going to try my master Herod's patience, especially today, when he's holding a party for his guests from Rome. Ah, man in the well, don't you know when to shut up? It's not a good idea to disturb the music of my master's gathering with that voice that calls to death – or so it seems to me, who doesn't understand his speech.

(She glances at her wristwatch.)

Ah, may my household gods protect me and keep me safe from harm, it's time to go and help Princess Salome put on her fine silks for the party, they'll cling to her reedlike body, that girl is a flesh-crazed woman, and I can't get rid of this bloodstain, even though I put plenty of Ajax Pine Forest in the water. It would be best to cover the stain with this carpet, I don't think my master will be happy to see bloodstains when he's having a party and, besides, the dancing girls' costumes will get soiled.

(She covers the stain with a carpet and trudges off.)

There's that man crying out again, like he's calling to death – or so it seems to me, poor, stupid Chaldean slave woman who doesn't understand the speech of this land of my masters. If he doesn't watch out, they'll call for the old executioner, that one with an obsession for knives. If he doesn't watch out.

With the Passing of Years Hairs Sprout

Well, if they were itching, he'd better cut them. They were tickling his nose. He switched on the horizontal light above the mirror. The light blinked and then grew steady. He contorted his face in order to emphasize his nose and glanced at himself sideways. Yes, they were poking out of his nose, he could see them. He opened the mirrored door of the bathroom cabinet and took out the small, curved scissors. Let's see now. He stuck his finger in his nose to push them further out. He stuck the hairs between the ends of the scissors and cut them. Off you go. Let's have a look at the other side. The bad thing was the more you cut them, the quicker and harder they grew. He pushed the others out with his finger and cut them as well.

Let's have a look at those ears. Unstoppable. He twisted his head in both directions. They kept growing and hanging further out. The bad thing was if he started on them, then there would be others. But he had to cut them, they looked like clumps of broom. His head seemed covered in hairs that, with the passing of the years, grew ever outwards. Better to cut them another day. There were barber shops where they cut them without even asking, while cutting your hair. Hairs all over the place. Like a werewolf. The more it fell off your head, the more it sprouted in other locations. How quickly the years passed, how obvious it looked. He put back the scissors and switched off the light.

Crime and Punishment

What have you been up to, with a face like that? You've been up to something, or you wouldn't look at me like that. You look like you've done something, you can't fool me. You look all guilty. It's the guilt that makes you lower your eyes. You know you can't fool me. I'm cleverer and stronger than you are. Who's in charge here, eh? Now tell me what you've done, you've been up to something. You can't fool me, I know you're trying to fool me. Don't cover it up, that'll just make matters worse. Tell me, confess your crime, and I shall be merciful with your punishment. You'll get a punishment, but I shall be just and merciful. Don't take too long about it, all you'll do is delay and aggravate the punishment. You don't want to tell me, eh? Is that it – you don't want to confess? Confess, and I'll take it into account. You won't say anything, that means I'm in the right. OK, you're forcing me to do this. You're forcing me to do this, you're asking to be punished. You know I don't like doing it, but you always make me. Always up to no good, why do you do it? Don't you realize I'll have to punish you? Always the same. Go on, bring me that rod. That's it, you're holding out your hands, you know what you have to do, there's no need for me to tell you. That's it, hold them out properly. I like it when you obey.

This is so you'll remember not to be naughty.

This is so you'll learn to confess your guilt.

This is so you won't force me to punish you any more.

This is so you won't do it again.

This is so you won't cry when you're punished.

This is so you'll remember I'm doing it for your own good.

This is so you'll learn.

This is so you'll pay for what you've done and find some peace.

Memory

'Roxelio!' His mother's voice calling to him from the kitchen made him feel snugger between the warm sheets. How lovely to have clean, ironed sheets. The ones in barracks were rougher to the touch. How well he felt. How many hours had he slept? His mother's smiling face peered around the half-open door. 'Come on, lazybones. You're going to spend the whole of your leave asleep!' She grabbed a slipper from the floor and made as if to beat him with it, he retreated under the sheets. 'Come on, you, breakfast is on the table.' He re-emerged just in time to glimpse his mother's scarlet dressing gown disappearing behind the door. He had to play a match with his friends that afternoon and take Charo dancing in the evening. He had to make the most of his leave. Would Charo feel like going to the river? He had to buy some condoms before playing the match. He got up, put on a green dressing gown and some slippers. He went out. In the kitchen, his wife was warming the coffee, gazing absentmindedly at the coffee pot on the gas stove. 'Has the boy shown you his marks?' she asked. He sat at the table behind her, stroked the edge of the porcelain cup with his fingers and said 'no'. Charo's slender figure ended in a head of dishevelled hair that was somewhere between blond and ash-grey. How thin she'd become with the years. Other women grew fat with the years and pregnancies, Charo had grown thinner. He passed his hands over the belly that spilled over his belt. She took the coffee pot off the stove, grabbed the milk carton in her other hand, turned around and poured first the milk, then the coffee into his cup. He added two spoonfuls of sugar and started stirring when he heard someone calling from the street, 'Roxelio!' He looked out, it was Fito and Mocos gazing upwards, holding their satchels. 'I'll be down in a minute,' he cried. He grabbed the sandwich that was on the table. 'Wait,' said his mother, 'wrap it in some paper, or you'll get your books dirty. Why do I always have to tell you?' He took the sheet of newspaper his mother held out and quickly wrapped the sandwich. He put the sandwich inside his satchel and raced out of the kitchen, imitating the sound of a car engine. The door on to the street banged. He slowly descended the stairs, holding on to the banisters with one hand and leaning on his stick with the other, 'slowly, Roxelio, slowly. You don't want to have a fall and break a bone as well. Old people's bones are like chicken's,' and he thought about poor Charo lying in bed, watching telly, with a broken hip. He stopped, took a breath, pulled out a handkerchief and wiped the corners of his mouth under his white moustache. He put away the handkerchief, breathed in deeply and started descending the stairs again, 'slowly, Roxelio, slowly. Old people are no use. How quickly life goes by.' When he reached the hallway, he saw Fito and Mocos, who were shouting, 'Let's go!' The three of them raced off, their satchels in one arm, the other held out like the wing of an aircraft, as they imitated the sound of an engine with their mouths. 'Vroom,' they went.

Ah, Pereira

Ah, hello. Come in, come in, I'm just finishing. Put it over there, on top of the sideboard. I'm glad you're here, Pereira, I've been so bored in the house on my own all day. Ever since Manolo went away, this house just hasn't been the same. Can you imagine, all the children married and settled, and me here on my own? Just when I'm most in need of my husband, he goes and dies. One is still young and in the mood for living. Ah, Pereira, what things you come up with. Ah, Xesús, I know you're just saying that to make me laugh. Get away with you! Ah, you're funny, you are. Behave yourself, Pereira, don't forget I'm a widow, stop fooling around. Ah, Pereira, please respect the fact this woman lost her husband less than a year ago. Ah, you do make me laugh. You're a naughty boy. I had no idea you could be so affectionate. Get off me, let go, Pereira, I'm all on my own, and someone might come in. Anyone could pass and hear what we're doing. Let go, let go, take your hand away from there, Pereira, if you tickle me, I'll roar out loud like a madwoman. Ah, goodness me, you're going to drive me crazy. What a lizard you are. Quieten down. Don't carry on like that. Ah, Pereira, I'll lose control, and you shouldn't take advantage. Ah, I do like it though, you pig. You shouldn't take advantage like that, I'm a widow, you thief. If Manolo were alive and saw us like this, he'd kill the two of us, he'd fly into a rage... Ah, what things you come up with. I even think I can still hear Manolo in the house, what nonsense I'm talking. Ah, my turtledove, you're going to kill me.

If your wife knew. If Milucha found out, she'd kill us. Carry on like that, just a little longer, I needed that. Ah, goodness me, the neighbours will hear. Please, Pereira, take care, or you'll kill me. Please, Pereira, you're a minx, taking advantage of the fact I'm all on my own. You're a little imp, you are, Pereira.

My Hand Calls to Memory

There's my hand, stroking my ear. I can't help it; if I'm not careful – and these days I'm not very careful – it rises up in silence and takes my ear. And then at once comes memory, melancholy Mnemosyne with her dog, and I'm full of memories, the dog prowling around outside.

They get clearer and clearer each day. It must be because they feel well with me, one comes and calls to the others. It must be because I don't put up much resistance to their actions. The day will come when they occupy the whole space inside me, that day I'll be brimful of memories. Full of that motionless past time. I can slowly feel the sweet, yellow lie filling the space inside me. Little by little, expelling life.

I don't pay any attention to what's before me. I sometimes go into a daze, not seeing or reading the page in front of me, succumbing to dumb memories. I have to summon all my strength in order to rouse myself from my reverie and seize the moment or the page. Seize the moment, each page that is there to be read. Little or much is the life I have left.

I sometimes wonder whether the memories I recall are real, if the things I remember really happened. Painful, sad memories. Sometimes even beautiful. But how can there be beautiful memories of painful childhood? Where is the merciless lucidity with which I once analyzed life? I have my suspicions that memory is one big lie. I have the impression that the balsam these memories seem to contain is just a seductive charm designed to win me over with its deceit. Sirens calling out to me, a static Odysseus. Sad, dry lucidity, my sister, come back, don't give in to the body's weakness.

Seize the moment, seize each page that is there to be read. I put down the pen and go to take my mid-afternoon medicines. Take them all carefully, in their proper order. Notice how the pills go down the dry throat with difficulty. How the thick syrup leaves a bittersweet taste in the mouth. These sensations are real. Focus on them. Prolong them.

(Manuscripts of ISIDRO PUGA PENA)

Philosophy

'He who speaks, sees, hears, does not doubt the senses, but we should doubt the senses, leave those who speak, see, hear, and doubt the senses, not speaking, seeing or hearing, like the three little monkeys that cover their mouths, eyes, ears, getting closer to real wisdom, which starts by not speaking, seeing or hearing, always doubting the senses, *in dubitate virtus* said the Latin or, if he didn't, then perhaps I saw or heard him say it, but he can't have paid much attention, he must have doubted the senses, doubted what he'd said, seen or heard, that is real wisdom, but how to believe in real wisdom without wondering whether it's false? And how to advance along the road of wisdom without being able to state what we think, see, hear, without being able to hear what we think, see, say, without being able to see what we think, see, hear? And how not to wonder whether the supposed advance along the road of wisdom really is an advance and really is on the road of wisdom? Isn't it really in what he speaks, sees, hears, speaking relentlessly, seeing restlessly, hearing deafeningly, without fear of speaking what is seen and heard, without fear of hearing what is spoken and seen, and without fear of seeing what is spoken and heard, leaving aside, not even glancing askance at the three little monkeys that cover their mouths, eyes, ears, one after the other, each in itself one, but indissolubly linked, making us see in consequence that we should doubt the senses, the only path to wisdom?'

'What was that again, what was that? I didn't get the last bit.'

'Something like – is the path of wisdom not really in what is spoken, seen and heard? More or less, something along those lines. It's a philosophy I came up with.'

(From the notebook *Philosophies* by MANEL)

My mother spoils me

I spoil my mother

My father hits me

I hit my father

I Bang on the Glass and Shout

It's hot, and the colours are electric. There's a vague sense of being in Africa, probably because of the number of black people, the heat, the old, dusty cars. There are four or five of us in an old car next to a lorry full of scrap metal. A motorbike ridden by two black people comes between the two vehicles. It's very dangerous, they're going to get killed. In effect, the motorbike and two passengers slam into a wall, fly over the wall. We stop to take a look.

Now there are two of us. We peer through a hole in the stone wall. The wall conceals some cliffs, down below is the sea. A beach with green waters and little depth. The bodies and remains of the motorbike are nowhere to be seen.

'That's right. Whenever people in an accident fall into the sea, they disappear,' says my male companion (or is it a female companion?).

People in coloured swimsuits bathe in the waters.

We sit down at the foot of some trees that create a dense space of ruby-coloured light. Probably the reflection of the leaves. It's very hot. The ground is like oilskin – ruby-coloured as well, but with spots. In reality, everything is covered in yellow spots, including the oilskin's upholstered door and golden handle a little bit further on.

'Shall we go and see?' says somebody (I don't know whether it's my male or female companion).

We go in. It's a forest of enormous trees, up above it's impossible to see the sky or treetops. It's pleasantly cool, there's no sound or wind. We pass through, and soon there's another door. We open it and see a room full of ruby-coloured boxes lined up on a table, stuffed with something like red potatoes dotted with holes. We feel an oppressive, damp heat on our faces. Probably coming from the potatoes. I turn back and close the door. Now, however, the room I'm in is small, full of old furniture and display cases, with a door on the far side.

My companion (definitely a man now, he looks young, but has a beard) and I decide to go through the door. We open it, and there's a dark forest of old trees. We notice above the door a sign that says 'Icelandic Forest'. We peer through. Right next to the door, half lost in the vegetation, is what looks like a man with a black, curly beard, almost a vegetable. It must be an imp, an imp from the Icelandic forest. We shut the door.

The room where we are now is clearly a laboratory illuminated by a window that lets in the light. 'Alchemists' Laboratory' says a sign hanging on the wall. Not a single alchemist is working at any of the four or five tables covered in glass vessels. A young woman dressed in light baggy clothes with golden embroidery and a white starched headscarf is standing and watching. I say to myself she resembles a Dutch woman from the sixteenth century, but I'm not really sure whether they dressed like that. She smiles and seems pleasant. I head towards the window, overcome by fear of what I might see. It appears we're on the third floor. Down below, between the bars, I see two men in uniforms and caps leaving the building, they must be security guards. I bang on the glass and shout. One of them stops and looks up. I gesture with my hands. He smiles and carries on walking. He goes away.

What will happen when night falls? I feel a hand on my shoulder: it's the Dutch woman, who says, 'Don't worry.' I wonder what's become of my companion.

'Where's the way out?'

'Over there,' she says, pointing in the direction of the room with the 'Icelandic Forest'. 'You go through the "German Forest" and then a library. There you'll see the exit.'

That may be true, but if it isn't and I enter that 'German Forest', then I may not be able to get back. There'll be somewhere else on this side.

'Where does that lead?' I point to a door that opens on to a dark corridor on one side of the room.

'You can't get out that way,' she says.

'But I want to go that way.'

'As you wish,' she says.

I look out of the window, but don't see anybody passing through the courtyard.

Doing a Pooh for Her

He watches his seven-month-old daughter attempt to do a pooh, she can't manage. Her tiny body contracts, her little face is red with pain. He'd like to help her, to save her the pain, but he can't. He can't go inside her and direct her inexperienced guts, intestines and sphincters, to help her do a pooh. He watches her sitting on the potty in the middle of the carpet, all alone, making a huge effort. He suffers and says to himself, while caressing his ear lobe, that a human being's radical solitude consists in this: that he can't do a pooh for her. Nobody can. That's what he thinks as he watches her exerting herself, all alone with her tummy ache. He feels an unexpected tear sliding down his cheek at the moment he understands she's also suffering. Love must be feeling the pain of the closeness of distinct, incommunicable solitudes, he thinks, gathering the tear with his finger. Ah, finally, the girl has managed to go and adopts an expression of relief. Love must also be feeling the joy he now feels. He again notices a tear on his face, it must be a different one.

COMMENTARY:

1.- Do you know how to locate the intestines and sphincters in a human body? Try.

2.- Do you know how and where tears are produced?

3.- What do you think of the author's definition of love? Have you ever felt something similar? When? Try to put what you felt into words.

4.- What impression do you have of solitude?

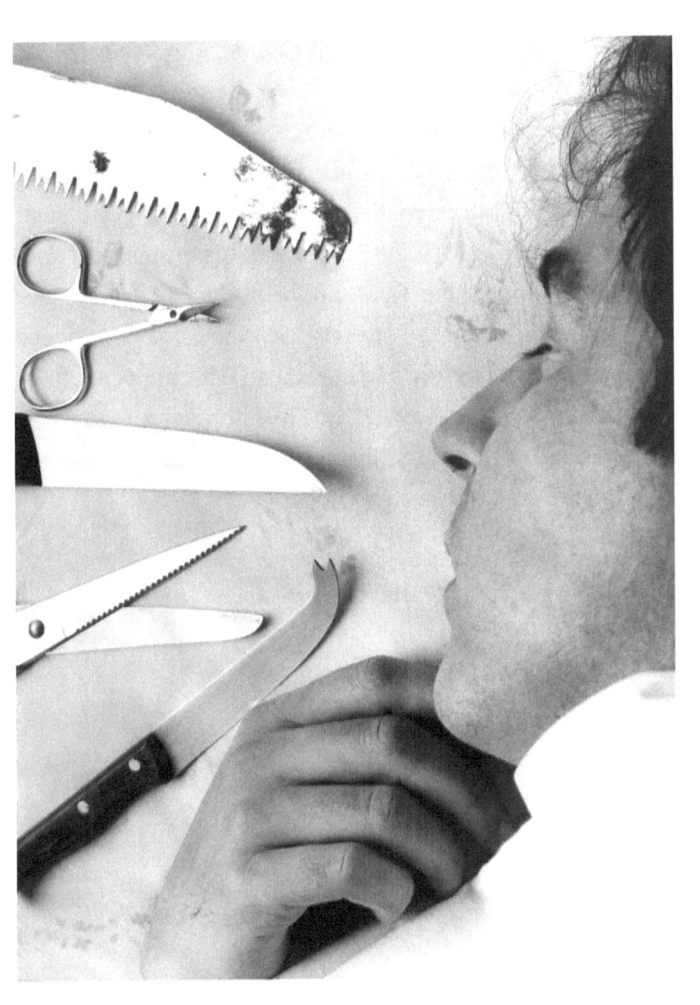

Driver

I'm a driver, driving my car, *conduzo o meu coche*, *conduzo o meu coche*, I head down the road, zoom past, *conduzo o meu coche*, zooooom.

I head down the road at night, my headlamps illuminate a man walking along with a plastic bag, I've gone past, but I know he's slowly thinking about his things, and now he deeply inhales the fresh air of night and looks over right at the lights on the other side of the estuary, as every night on his way home, and carries on walking peacefully because he's going home, but I've stopped already and am heading in that direction, driving my car, *conduzo o meu coche*, *conduzo o meu coche*.

Third Sorrowful Mystery

THE TYRANNY OF DNA

The thing I like best is being quiet, being like this, chatting away, thinking of my things, without doing anything. And yet I'm often overwhelmed by a desire to go far away from here, for good. That's how it is; as philosophy says, we're both one thing and its opposite. Or something like that. Positively, I read that somewhere. The point is, in the end, I let my desire subside, I stay where I am and carry on chatting away. I prefer to be quiet than to take off somewhere. And yet I often wonder what would happen to me if I did take off and see the world or decide to start working at something. I don't know, as a waiter or a sales rep. I often wonder about that and imagine myself as a sailor holding on to the gunwale with my peaked cap and a pipe in my mouth, with a white braided jacket, bow tie and tray in the café of a hotel, or dressed in a suit and tie, waiting at a doctor's surgery with my folder. I'm sometimes afraid these other Nanos in my head may really exist. You never know with such things. I don't believe in witches, but exist – they exist. Thought has great strength; the word, which is just expressed thought, even more so. You can't play with words; once they're out, you can't retrieve them. So I'm afraid of saying such things because, once I say them, the other Nano I possibly wanted to be might suddenly turn up, and such things fill me with dread. But since I'm sitting here quietly, not moving or doing anything, just talking, well, I can't stop thinking about the things I might have been, the people I might have turned into. I could have been a doctor, a carpenter, a landscape painter, a teacher, a gardener... it makes me very sad not to have been all those things. I feel loneliness. One can be so many things, and they're all so interesting, it's a shame not to be them. Of course, this is only if you start thinking about them, otherwise nothing. The time has passed for me, I'll soon be forty-five, which is quite an age. Or was it fifty-five? I don't know, I can't remember. I'll have to remember to ask my mother. The years just fly by. Time kills one without one realizing, one gradually withers away, shrivels up like a raisin. Like a willy, which is no longer the same. This has been scientifically proven, mine used to get hard more often and for longer periods. The average has changed. When I was younger, I used to have to give it a beating, and another, and another – as often as six times, so it would calm down. The little weasel wouldn't let me sleep. Now I do a handjob every three days, and that's me sorted. Only because I remember, eh, it's not as if it stands up and says, 'Here I am!' Time also does for willies. Nothing is immune to the passage of time. Immune means you can't hurt it. What I mean is if you're not immune, then you're open to attack. Willies are not immune. Everything expires, and if you don't believe me, just have a look at milk and yoghurts. It's a relief, by the way, it caused me no end of suffering going around with a stiffy. I only had to see a woman two kilometres away, and bam – a-tten-tion!! It was a real suffering, a form of slavery. Because, right, you're in the mood, but there's almost always nothing you can do about it, and that's where the suffering comes in. I reckon most of the traumas and frustrations men have are for this reason. They're always running around after pussy like a pack of hounds. Now that's what

I call a misfortune, a calamity. Why want what you can't have? That leads to the frustrations and traumas many men have. If only we could cut off our member, that would put an end to a lot of problems. I've written on this subject in a notebook called *Knife-Grinder and Gelder's Manual*. There's just no way to deal with it. I still get like that, and I'm sixty-five! Or was it fifty-five? I can't remember, I'll have to ask my mother. Well, I still get that inflammation down below, and it makes me suffer because, you know, you can't go around bothering women, asking every woman you see, 'Excuse me, madam, would you mind extending me a little relief?' or something along those lines, because you'll get a slap in the face, quite rightly, women are almost never thinking about dirty things, so suppose she's thinking about something else – a child with a cold, for example – she's thinking about something else, and you go up with your problem, well, she's going to give you a slap in the face. She does well, that kind of thing really bothers them. The point is we'd all be much better off if the desire never presented itself. Desire just leads to problems because, if you put a lot of desire together – I mean a shedload of desire – you end up doing something stupid. And if you do something stupid, then you get into trouble. I've studied myself and, in order to avoid problems, so this willy won't govern my life and I won't have to depend on women, I've come up with a method. You see, I think about things. There are those who claim, 'Boh, Nano's stupid, he's no use,' and so on, but that's not true. The fact is I think about important things, and leave the rest to others. For example, this hasn't been discovered yet, but I know we men all have a bug inside. It couldn't be any other way, we're always crazy for women. We men are capable of anything. I sometimes think about myself and feel afraid. I wonder if we're not made of the same stuff as the Bogeyman. Though the Bogeyman may just be a dream. That said, when you read what's in the papers... Like that business about the seven-year-old girl who turned up dead the other day, all the things that had been done to her, it's better not to think about it. All because of a bug we carry around like a condemnation. There's another bug that's similar, it's called a tapeworm, but what that does is make you want to eat. This must be a 'gapeworm', which makes you hanker after women. That beast is a danger for us and for women. I think about things that are important. Some day, a Japanese investigator will turn up and discover this bug, but in the meantime, nobody believes me; if I go and tell somebody, they just say, 'That Nano's not right in the head.' Well, they can go and eat shit for all I care. I find things out and come up with inventions. For example, a method so you can control your willy, and not the other way around. I reckon that's something really, really fundamental. Well, here it is. The method has a preventative part, that's pretty fundamental, this is something that is becoming more and more popular in medicine: prevention. Prevention consists in this: the patient has to control his sexual rhythm – I call it 'sexirrhythm' – and get ahead of the game. So for example, if his thing gets hard every two days, then he has to relieve himself always a day earlier. Should somebody in this situation see he gets an erection on even days, then he has to start relieving himself on an odd day, before he gets the erection, I'm not sure if you understand. Then he must carry on, without rest, every odd day. To start with, it may not want to, so you have to provoke it, to do it even if you don't want to. The point is to do it when you decide, not when your member decides. That's the difference. In this, as in so many other things, the point is to know who's in charge. You, or the penis. There's a second part, which is used to confront your dick when it gets out of hand. The method may seem a little brusque, but I assure you it's scientific. It consists in a piece of cord. You take a piece of cord and tie said member with it. You follow? Then you pull the cord out the top of your trousers and slip it in a pocket. Should the thing get inflamed, you stick your hand in your pocket, and wham! You'll soon see how it goes down. Look, I have a cord here, it comes out here and then goes in my left pocket, that's my good hand. Whenever I need it, wham! Ow! I always pull a little too hard. Ow, ow! That hurt. But you see, in this way I can be talking to a woman and still remain in control of the situation. If I see things are getting a little out of hand, then wham, down it goes. There are times I'm with a woman, and wham! They're always saying, 'Oh, Nano, what's the matter? You look all funny.' Of course I do, it hurts. But I keep quiet and pretend it's a tic. The important thing is I'm in charge. If I lose control, my member will be in charge, and one will end up doing something stupid. If you do something stupid, then you land in trouble. Better to cut it off. Those who want to have children should rush off and make them – one, two, three, four – and then snip! Call in the castrator. Worry no more. It may give pleasure, but the pleasure is the same as the problems. Or else the problems are more. Though even that wouldn't work. I bet you'd then feel a phantom penis. When something dies, the phantom remains. It'd still be there, even if it wasn't. And I bet it would still get inflamed. Except now you wouldn't be able to get it down. The torture would be greater. Like this hand of mine that's missing. I bet you can't tell it's made of plastic. I bet it looks like the other, eh? German. German hands are the best, though there are also American and Italian ones. American ones are useless, they don't get the colours to match. They had a black one in their catalogue. For black people, obviously. They were prepared to let me have it at a reduced price, but I don't think that would have been suitable... Then there are the Italian ones, which are very cute, they look a bit like a woman's, they're smaller, but since the hand I have left is actually quite big, I went for a German one, which fitted me better. The brand is very good, it's called *Die gute Hand*. It was more expensive, but my mother said, 'Don't worry, son, I always taught you to wash your hands and cut your nails, so now I want you to carry on looking like my child.' And she went and bought it. I'm happy with it, it's not the real one, obviously. If I think about it, the whole thing comes back to me, and I feel nostalgic. If it were today, they'd sew it back on, but there was none of that twelve years ago. Besides, if you lose a hand out at sea, as happened to me, you can't do anything about it until you return to port. I sometimes feel it itching, even though it's not there. The doctor warned me, 'You'll carry on noticing it, as if it were still there. There are times it will hurt or itch... as if you still had it. This is your phantom hand, the one that doesn't leave.' Well, I'm just glad this phantom thingy allows me to have a rubber hand in its place and doesn't mind. A phantom is like a memory of the hand. When you lose something, the memory is left behind. Memory is like an artificial hand. A prosthesis, as it's called. That's right. My goodness, how complicated it is to live. Less life, more memory. Memory is something like death, but life is something that bursts in all directions, and there's no way of picking up the pieces, they're scattered all over the place, and one doesn't know what to choose. The only things that are certain are the passage of time and the Bogeyman, who doesn't leave, he's always there. I know this because of my dreams. I don't like falling asleep because of my dreams. Sometimes one doesn't know how one keeps one's head in the midst of all this life. And what about children? I don't know how they don't go crazy. Their father this, their mother that... and so on. A mound of frustrations and traumas, I studied it in a book, childhood is when you get the most traumas and frustrations. You get them all the time, in abundance. We pay very little attention to children. I sometimes jot things down, especially when they have to do with philosophy. I have a notebook full of philosophical things that occur to me. I thought something had to be done for children, and so I started writing things for them. Stories, stuff like that. I've written the whole Bible out in rhyming couplets –

'Cain and Abel, they looked at him, one looked well, the other was grim', and so on. The Trojan War as well, the adventures of Odysseus, king of the Greeks. Stories, the life of Rosalía de Castro, a play by that Englishman that tells of a prince whose father was killed and so he goes and kills his stepfather... Uff, I've got notebooks full of scribblings. But I don't know whether anyone will want to publish them. If I was in contact with an editor, I'd tell him my idea, I have some very good ones. The thing is he may not be all that interested. Probably not. Given there are other people more famous than me. There's a local lad here called Roque Morteiro who first worked as a waiter and then produced a detective or an adventure story, I can't remember. He must have had some connection or other that dictated the novel to him, I'll have to ask him some day. I've also written about the men I've met with the largest penises, I called it *What the Dickens!* One guy had this penis that was as large as a jar of Nutella or Nesquik. You needed two hands just to hold it. Enormous beast. Like a jar of Nutella. Another guy had a penis that was as long as a Revilla sausage. His name was Francisco, and he came from Coruña. He would charge to show it off and, since there were always people who didn't believe it when you told them, old Francisco made quite a business. We would say, 'Come on, Francisco, show us your Revilla,' and he would say, 'First show me your money.' We'd throw in a couple of coins, five pesetas each, he would roll it out and lay it on the table. A real Revilla sausage. As everybody gazed on in astonishment, he would rake in the money. The saddest thing about this lad was that he was afraid of women. Imagine that, with all the success he could have had – there are always those who like a bit more material – he was afraid of them. It turns out, when he was little, an uncle of his, who'd had an operation in that region, told him how, walking along a path one day, he'd bumped into a fairy. A fairy is a woman with red hair and clear eyes that lives by a spring or some old rocks. Well, he'd bumped into a fairy, and the fairy had said if he was willing, then so was she. To start with, his uncle had got the shivers when he saw her, but he soon warmed up. He went to where the fairy lived, in a cave in the mountain, and there they did it. She gave him a gold coin and told him never to tell anybody because, if he did and she found out about it, she would have to punish him. He didn't listen and boasted about his adventure in the village. A few days later, the fairy appeared on the same path and proposed doing it again. So off they went. But just as the sparks were flying and he was getting most excited, she went and said, 'Didn't I tell you if you talked about it, I'd have to punish you?' At this point, he felt teeth chomping on his willy. Well, that's exactly how it was. The poor man was bleeding when he got back to the village, where they did what they could to cure him. Can you imagine such a story? Who would have believed such a thing? Well, poor old Francisco heard about this as a child, got the jitters and didn't want to know any more about the matter because of what had happened to his uncle. A couple of years ago, I bumped into him, he was fat and balding, and I asked him, 'What then, Francisco?

You done it yet?' He said he hadn't, the whole idea made him sick. You can see that was a trauma. A real frustration. The fact is we men are not very immune to traumas. We have lots of problems and complications. So much obsession means we're not much good for anything. It shouldn't be like that, but it is.

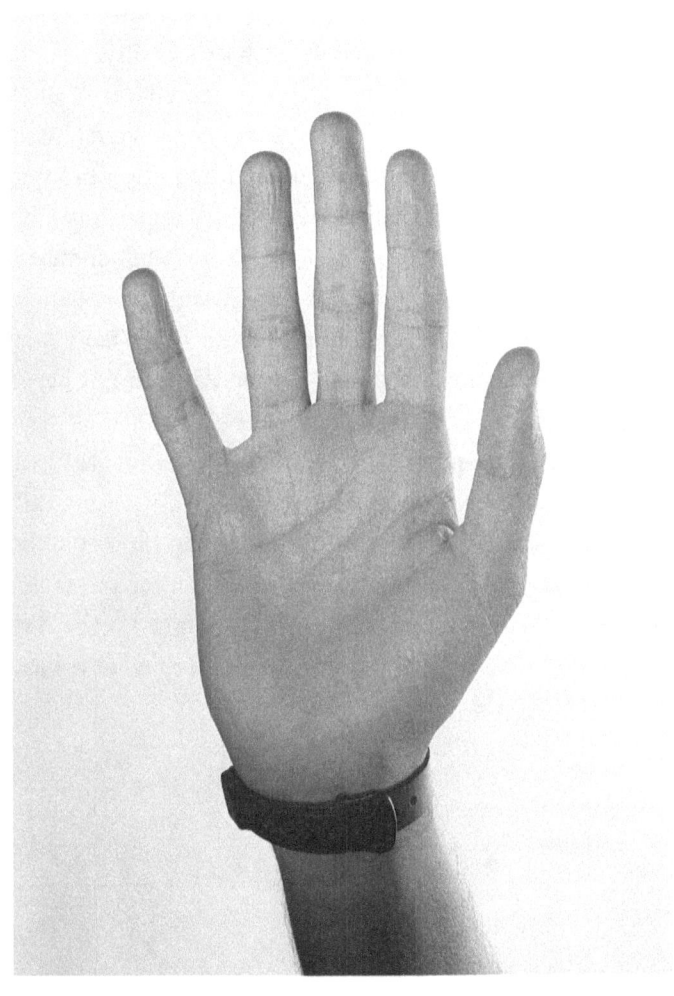

Photo

This one here is my cousin Fernando, who died in Bilbao, he fell off some scaffolding. And that's Nucho, who is a civil guard in Barcelona, he got married to a woman from Seville. A very pretty one, too. This photo of me was taken the day my nephew Paco got married. That pretty woman there belonged to the wife's family. I think her name was Amparo. This girl here – pretty, isn't she? – well, she had a very bad life. She married a wretch who caused her all sorts of problems. It turned out a brother then killed him, the brother went and hanged himself, and I don't know what else. A real disaster. She's married to a travelling salesman now, I think. And her situation has improved. Here's Nano in a suit and tie. What a son I had! I don't know what he'll do the day I'm not here. That was on my brother Xosé's name day, when he was celebrating the baptism of his little boy, Andrés. Andrés is now quite grown up. He was a pretty little thing, all round and squidgy like a bun. It's amazing how quickly the years go by. You only realize when you look at these photos. Just a couple of months to go before I retire. I'd carry on if I could, but my concentration isn't what it was. We're getting old.

Aaah

'Uuum.'

'Ah.'

'Uuum. Mmm.'

'Like that.'

'Aih. Mmm.'

'You like it?'

'Mmm. Yeah.'

'Auum, that's lovely. Aah.'

'Mmm.'

'Grrr, grrr.'

'Uuhuuuh. How lovely. Uumm.'

'Aah, aaah, ahaah. Take that.'

'Ouuh, uuumm, mmm. You're killing me, mmm. That's lovely, mmm.'

'Aaah, ahaah, ahaah, take that, aah, all of it, aah.'

'Aiii, aiii, augh. Don't, you're killing me. Uuuum. You're going to kill me.'

'Aah, ahaah, ahaah, I'm dying, aaah.'

'Auh. Ummm.'

'I'm dead.'

True Love

He was so happy he almost skipped along the street. She was so pretty. He almost couldn't believe that she liked him. Did she really love him? She might. She certainly liked him. Yes, but was she in love with him? Certainly not the way he was in love with her. He would have given his life for her. Were she to put him to the test, he would have done anything. Anything, whatever she asked. Anything, throw himself into the sea, under a train, anything. He would have defended her in all circumstances. Had they attacked her, a gang or something, he would have turned up, pin, pas, karate kick, pick up a stick, pamba, pamba, deal out a real beating, he would. He would have mown down anyone in the way. He really loved her. And she liked him, he almost couldn't believe it. He would never be this happy again in all his life. She was so pure. She was like a picture-book fairy with her long hair falling over her shoulders and down her back, surrounded by this golden light or something. Ana was like a poem. He would write her a poem. A poem that talked of her golden hair, her eyes green as seaweed, as a lemon tree's new leaves, her lips red as ripe apples just waiting to be bitten, her breasts, her breasts, aah, how he loved her. She was so fair and pure. Today he would ask her for a kiss. He was so happy he almost skipped along the street.

Aaah

'Take that. That's it. Suffer. Enjoy, you bitch. Like that, like that. Take that, and that. And that. You like it, eh? You like it. Well, take that. And that. Like that, like that. Hold on there. What is it, eh? You suffering, eh? Take that, you bitch, ai. Aah.'

'Aii, please, you're killing me. Aii, please. You're destroooying me, aii, I can't take any more. You're crushing me, killing me, aah. What do you think you're doing, you're killing me, aaah. That's it, more, all of it, all of it, finish me off, aah. You're killing me, aah.'

Doll

This is the story of something that happened when I was on board ship in the Gran Sol, I was there for a period. That was where I lost my hand. It's the description of something that happened to me and makes one think we people are very complicated and difficult to understand. Sometimes we should make more of an effort to comprehend our peers, that is all the others.

On board ship, there are all sorts of shenanigans. We'd spent a week at sea, a week rolling around, the waves crashing against the boat, splashing salt water everywhere. A north-easterly was blowing. That was when Eladio of Camariñas got out the doll. He opened a suitcase, took out some folded, coloured pieces of plastic, took out a pump for inflating air beds, plugged it in and started blowing up the pieces of plastic. And so the doll was inflated. We all laughed at the idea. We always had dirty mags with us at sea. But he suggested a ride with her for a hundred pesetas. 'Uuuh,' we all said. But one of us handed over the money right away: Paco da Serra. That guy was a real brute. He grabbed the doll and went over to the corner. We all laughed and egged him on, 'Go on, Paco, her legs are wide open, go on, Paco, she's in the mood,' stuff like that. But he turned around with a look of satisfaction and handed the doll back to Eladio, 'There she is. Go on, laugh, I've had my fill,' and he coughed up the hundred pesetas. Eladio asked whether anyone else wanted a go. We all said no, so he went and washed the doll, and then expelled the air.

The days went by, and gradually we all stepped up, being stuck on board, nowhere to go, you can imagine. On board ship, there are all sorts of shenanigans. The point is we all had a go with Mari. That was the name Eladio gave her. One day, I was there, I'd just been working up on deck, when Petete came over and said he'd buy the doll from Eladio, he wanted it for himself. Eladio said it wasn't for sale, he got more money by loaning her out. Petete said, 'Name your price.' So Eladio, who was a natural-born thief, said, 'Twenty-five.' For twenty-five thousand, you could do whatever you liked, that doll can't have been worth more than five or ten. Well, he asked for twenty-five. And Petete went and gave it.

People thought Petete planned to carry on with the business, but I realized this wasn't the case. Some others asked to have a go, but he said no. People thought he was making them wait so he could demand a higher price. But no, I realized this wasn't the case. Petete had grown fond of the doll. He was a little strange. He'd been in prison for smuggling drugs and almost died of a gunshot wound he received from a policeman when holding up a chemist's. He was one of those walking disasters who go stumbling through life, there are lots of people like that. He wasn't a bad guy to have on board, he chatted to everybody, but kept his secrets pretty much to himself, he wasn't one of those who devised or got up to mischief, but he was a good guy to have around.

One day, he came off deck and went looking for his doll, which he kept in his kit bag, but it wasn't there. The man got really desperate. We all tried to calm him down.

'Calm down, Petete, you must have put it somewhere else,' stuff like that. But the guy was crazy, he wouldn't listen. At this point, that brute Paco da Serra turned up with the doll and said with a laugh, 'I went to have it off with your girlfriend.' Petete was as quick as a flash and, before we knew it, he'd got out his knife for chopping bait and stabbed Paco da Serra three times. Several of us jumped on top of him, it took all of us to hold him down. The guy was crazy. Can you imagine? All of this on account of a doll. But that's people for you. Everyone is their own world, and who knows what traumas and frustrations they carry inside?

And the moral of the story is: we people are pretty complicated. More than you might think.

(From Nano's notebook *Concerto for the Left Hand*)

Aaah

The two mammals are knotted together (on top of the bed), the male on his knees behind the female, who is on all fours. He rubs his stiff penis against her buttocks and grabs a breast in each hand. She twists around and turns to seek out the male's gaze. They look at each other, she sticks out her tongue and wiggles it. He grabs the female by the buttocks and inserts his penis, starting to make rhythmical movements back and forth, back and forth. She writhes in the male's grip, he holds her tits, her eyes are closed. He grabs her by the waist now and starts pummelling her, his eyes closed as well. He collapses on top of her, and the movements of the male mammal's pelvis grind to a halt. They remain in a tight knot/embrace for several moments.

Take a Look

I wanted you to take a look, doctor. To check I'm clean, doctor. My husband has his way with a pig, doctor, and then he comes to me, doctor, I don't want him to. I'm clean and I'm afraid of catching some disease, doctor, my husband is a real pig. That's why I wanted you to take a look, doctor, I've never had a problem down there, doctor, and I don't want to catch something now, doctor, my husband comes to me after he's been with that pig. I'm not a pig, doctor, and I'm afraid of catching something. For a man to go with just anybody, doctor, even with a pig, well, that's disgusting. When I give it its food, doctor, it's horrible just to watch it eat, doctor, it's so eager it's frightening. Perhaps it's that eagerness that turns my husband on, doctor, a man is like an animal. When I hear them out in the sty, doctor, when I hear it squealing like that, doctor, I remember the day it gave birth and then gobbled up its little piglets, doctor. It's so eager it's frightening, doctor, it gobbled up its own babies, doctor. When I hear it squealing with my husband in the sty, doctor, well, I start thinking about its little piglets. I wanted you to take a look, doctor, to check I'm clean, doctor. I'm afraid I may suffer from the same eagerness, doctor. Go on, take a look.

Mortuary Botany

The scanty diet of an old man sick in body and mind offers constant illuminations about life. When the effect of the tranquillizers wears off, in that phase when the mind wakes up and delirium has yet to take control, just now as I'm writing, it seems to me I'm filled with wisdom. As if really all the books I've read, all the papers I've written – or rather all the papers and books I've lived – were my life in some way, as if all that mortuary work enabled me to comprehend life.

With this look illuminated by the combined effect of tranquillizers and amphetamines, I see the apple I have to sate my slender appetite has a worm. I think about that worm and whether it entered the apple one day or was already there. I wonder whether all apples are born with a worm inside them.

I also feel a worm inside me, gnawing away, and fear the day it gnaws right through me and gets to the other side. I'm afraid of coming face to face with this worm. I'd like to know whether I was born with it, whether we are all born with a worm inside us.

Truly the observation of nature provides true knowledge. I think I'm going to eat the apple, and the worm as well.

(Manuscripts of ISIDRO PUGA PENA)

Arte Cisoria

Blow in this eye, I have a mote. / This letter has been sent by a Colombian friar and has to travel around the world. / Don't laugh, don't laugh, it'll only get worse. / Heaven does not exist, but hell does. / There's the girl who sells sweets at the traffic lights. / A perpetual sacrifice to placate an endless voraciousness. / It's just that teacher has it in for me. / Don't fail to do what it asks and, once you've read it, say three Our Fathers and three Hail Marys. / Your supper's in the oven. / *Son espía.* / 'Like that. Slowly.' 'Doesn't it hurt?' / Francisco Manuel made 27 copies, sent them out within nine days, and immediately an uncle of his in Caracas died and left him 25 million. / Canst thou not minister to a mind diseased, pluck from the memory a rooted sorrow, raze out the written troubles of the brain and with some sweet oblivious antidote cleanse the stuff'd bosom of that perilous stuff which weighs upon the heart? / I wonder if they'll finally do it. They pretend to do it, but don't actually do anything at all. In this country, it's always the same. / Why, instead of shitting on Christ, don't you shit on God? After all, he's the one who gave his son that life of his. / To be quite honest, I'm a bit of a liar. / Knife-griiiiinder, umbrella-meeeeender. / Sunflower seeds, tiger nuts, sweets. Sugared almonds as well. / I'll send you some chrysanthemums, God dammit. Ones that have been cut from under a hanged man.

The Iliad for Children

OK, so the point was there was a king called Menelaus, who was king of Troy. He was capricious when he was a little boy and wanted everything he set eyes on. Monkey see, monkey do. Everything for him. But of course you can't always have everything and, when he didn't get it, he'd burst into tears. Cry like a little baby. He was lacking nothing, his parents bought everything for him. 'Don't cry, little thing, don't cry.' And that was how they brought him up to be selfish and capricious.

Once he'd grown up, well, of course he liked women and jumped on top of them like a dog. You'll see this when you grow up, you'll see what people are like, some of them are like dogs. Then again, you may already know this, children are introduced to this kind of nonsense at school. OK, so the point was this Menelaus, one day he caught sight of a very pretty woman who went by the name of Helen. He became obsessed with her and wanted her for himself. 'Come to me, girl,' he said. Helen was a bit flirtatious, but she knew how to get what she wanted. You can look, but not touch. She said uh-uh, she was married to the king of the Greeks, who was called Odysseus, so no way. Ooh, you can imagine what a fuss Menelaus made, he had to have her. So he picked her up and took her away. Well, that really put the cat among the chickens. You see, that was the start of the Trojan War.

Of course, you can imagine how Odysseus reacted when he found out his wife had been abducted. There's a saying according to which you should never lend anybody your wife or your fountain pen. Of course, there weren't any fountain pens back then. So Odysseus went and cried out, 'Let Troy burn!' He put together a huge army of soldiers, ships, catapults, anything he might need, and set out for Troy with the aim of conquering it.

The Greek army arrived. But the city – Troy was a city, even though it had a king – the city had these enooormous, taaall, toooowering waaaalls. There was no way of getting in to conquer it. To make matters worse, Menelaus would appear on top of the walls and make fun of the Greeks. The Greeks would get really annoyed because there was nothing they could do about it.

This had been going on for several years when a Greek general who went by the name of... Dammit, I mean darn it, Odysseus was the Greek general, he wasn't the king. The king of the Greeks was... was... Well, blow me down, I can't remember. Not Achilles. Nope, it's not going to come to me. Doesn't matter, I'll remember later. So it turned out this Odysseus was a cunning sort of chap, cunning means he was as sly as a fox. You see a fox has to be sly in order to catch the chickens. Sly means very clever, very on the ball. So this Odysseus went and said, 'Let's play a trick on them. Listen up. Why don't we make a huge wooden horse on wheels, hop inside with a hundred warriors and then tell the Trojans we're leaving, we can't conquer Troy, so we give up? When they come out of the city, they'll see the horse, take a liking to it, and I bet you they'll roll it inside, that way at night we can come out of the horse and conquer Troy. Eh? What do you think?' The others nodded and said they would do it.

They made the horse, Odysseus and a hundred Greek warriors hid inside, and told the Trojans they were leaving. That was exactly what they did: they struck camp and removed the catapults so they could see it was true they were leaving. The Trojans, well, you can imagine how happy they were to see the back of the Greeks. 'They're really leaving,' Menelaus couldn't believe his eyes. Helen probably felt a bit sad because, if Menelaus was a spoilt brat before that, you can imagine what he'd be like after pulling one over on the Greeks. Helen may have got used to living in Troy. Or perhaps she was a bit afraid that her husband, that king of the Greeks whose name won't come to me, might think she'd gone off with Menelaus out of choice and want to give her a beating. There's sometimes a lot of macho behaviour and mistreatment in marriages.

The point was that the Trojans came out of their walls, saw this large, pretty horse standing there and said, 'Hey, that's pretty. Look what the Greeks have left us. Obviously it wouldn't fit inside their ships, so they've left it behind.' They brought it inside their city, which was exactly what Odysseus wanted. 'In we go!' After that, well, of course the Trojans had themselves a huge party, the war was over. There was dancing, tambourines, pies and wine. I'll pay for this round, Johnnie boy will pay for another... until they could barely stand. By the time they were all under the influence, drunk as lords, so blind they couldn't see straight, well, night had fallen, and out came Odysseus and his friends. You can imagine what followed. They conquered the lot of them. They seized them all, Menelaus included. Helen as well. And took over the city.

That was how the Greeks won the Trojan War. Troy burned as a result, which is why we have the expression 'Troy will burn, God dammit', which is more or less the same as saying the shit is going to hit the fan. Odysseus left for his homeland, which was an island. And that was the end of the Trojan War. There was this poet, Omar, who told the whole story in verse. And that was that.

Ah, now I remember. The king of the Greeks was called Agamemnon, Agamemnon, that was it. I remember now. I know this story off by heart. I like it because it suggests that brain is better than brawn.

(From Nano's notebook *Stories I Like Best*)

Dermatology

He pretended not to hear the first time I asked him to lower his trousers. He was ashamed to be examined by a woman. His legs were hairy and spindly.

'Your pants as well. I have to examine your penis.'

He slowly lowered his pants. They were clean. He had a long penis with an ample foreskin. He remained still, with his arms at his sides and his eyes on the floor. He felt uncomfortable with his trousers down, revealing his genitals.

I took a paper napkin and a cotton bud and approached him. He shuffled on his feet.

'Please would you retract your prepuce so I can see the glans.'

'What do you want me to do?'

'Pull back your foreskin.'

He gently pulled it back with both hands, as if doing it slowly were more polite. He carried on holding his penis in both hands and looked at me from above, then at his hands and penis.

I moved the glans from side to side with the cotton bud. There were traces of sperm and dirt at the base, it showed ulceration and a wound with papules. There was also the scar of a chancre that had healed some time ago. Was this that woman's husband? Was this the one that went with the pig that gobbled up its piglets? I had seen him before in bars with other men. He was young and handsome. Was it possible he'd mounted a pig? What are men really like?

'Doctor.'

What motivates men? What drives them to mount a woman or a pig? Is it the same driving force in both situations? What are men like, what impels them?

'Doctor.'

'What?'

'Is there something wrong with me?'

'Aha.' I stood up and threw the cotton bud and paper napkin into the pedal bin.

I went back behind my desk.

'You have a small infection provoked by bacteria. Probably some kind of relation you've had with someone or something that wasn't very clean. I'm going to prescribe you an ointment to apply straightaway and I'm going to refer you to a specialist. You need to see a dermatologist who can take a proper look. You can pull up your pants and trousers now, we don't want you catching a cold.'

'Yes, ma'am,' he turned around in a gesture of modesty, his shirt tail obscuring his buttocks, and slowly got dressed.

Arte Cisoria

A shareholder sent out 27 copies and received 270,000 pesetas. General Rospiito in the Philippines lost his wife seven days after breaking the chain. / There are hamburgers made of meat. / Blessed are those who suffer. / You are different. You don't give, you take. I could love you to death. / Later on he sent the 27 copies and was overjoyed to find his wife safe and sound, despite having been retained by political terrorist action in those parts. / 'Mac, you ever been in love?' 'No, I've been a bartender all my life.' / If what you want is to blaspheme, then do it properly. Don't lay into the victim, rise up against the executioner. / Face me, turn around, don't move your hands, don't move your feet. / Your breakfast is on the table. Close the door when you leave. / And that smell of hair tonic? / There's no beauty here, only death and decay. / Precious in the sight of the Lord is the death of his saints. / Observe your luck for 24 days after sending the copies, trust in the Lord with all your heart and everything will turn out OK. / I don't know whether I told you, you can deceive anybody except the deaf and blind. You can't deceive them because they won't let you. / Knives, scissors, to grind! / I can't remember now the words to that song about dead children. And I'm not going to. / I want to feed you with my own hand, to feed you with my mouth. So you'll love me and follow me everywhere. / Send the copies out and in 24 days you'll get a pleasant surprise. It's been proven. But don't hold on to it for more than nine days. / It was late, so I went to the cinema without you.

My Sex (Pear-Shaped Piece)

I move my hand, slowly, move my hand, slowly does it. There it goes, there it goes. Aaah. I cover the head with my hand, aaaah, aah. That's it. *'Tis a consummation devoutly to be wished.*

I open my eyes and gaze at my hand grasping the point. I carefully take it away and open it, forming a bowl. The juice gradually descends over the wrinkles, over the lines – of life, fortune, love. I stretch out my arm and contemplate the motionless substance sitting in the cup of my hand. *Whether 'tis nobler in the mind?* It has the sad appearance of condensed milk, but I know it doesn't taste sweet, it tastes bitter. I lift my hand to my nose and sniff that misleading scent of sea, what false seas inhabit us, what a sinister ocean it is from which we draw those inverted rivers that run past our stomachs, leaving bathyal smells on our pelvises. I gaze at that moving message in my hand, written millions of times, millions of times, life is implacable, life is implacable, life is implacable. And there's nothing I can do about it. Nothing I can do to resist the orders that hold sway inside. Inside somewhere. You feel the sign, glinting away, an electric discharge that tickles, and you know it wants more, it's eager for more, and there's nothing you can do about it, it's only going to grow in intensity, control your hand, you'll have to grab hold of that blind doll that leads you ever onwards, ever onwards, until it finds a hidey-hole, and you don't want to let it, so you try tricking it, come and hide in my hand, come on, pretty boy, this hand loves you, and you'll have to give it all your love until you draw out sluggish slurps of abundance, *'tis a consummation devoutly to be wished.* Amazed, you'll notice a gap where you have been robbed, another gap. That message will be there again, the same message you contemplate in your hand. But you're not going to give it free rein, not even down the toilet. So you grab a piece of toast from on top of the table, spread the substance clinging to your hand all over it, and rub your hand. Now you fold the toast in two and eat it. Ummm, ummm. You notice the cold taste. That freshness that goes back inside, far inside, penetrating the surface of that sea, plush, passing through abyssal, bathyal layers until it settles on the bottom. That bottom from where another signal arrives. Oh no. Not again.

(From the manual *Know Thyself: Self-Sufficiency*, chapter 3, 'Handiwork', by M. W. WILLIAMS)

Dead Hand

First, he felt something like an itch, not much at all. But then it started hurting. When he removed the rubber hand, he saw his fingers were sprouting again. Growing from the stump.

He mentioned it to the owner of the orthopaedic shop where he'd bought the hand. 'Ah, that happens sometimes. Don't worry, I'll sort it out for you.' He pulled a wooden board from under the counter, took his hand and placed it on the board. He then brought out, also from under the counter, a large knife and cut off the nascent fingers. 'There you go. Now you'll have to put on a bandage. You can use your orthopaedic hand again in a week. And should the need ever arise, don't hesitate to come back with confidence.'

That was two months ago. He'd felt the itching again two days ago. But he didn't want to go back to the shop.

(From Nano's notebook *Dreams and Occurrences*)

Prometheus Gets Angry at Zeus' Refusal to Let Men Have Fire So They Can Reach the Summit of Their Civilization

'God dammit!'

Arte Cisoria

They're ugly words, bad words, that shouldn't be said. / Do it the way you're supposed to: conscientiously. Shit on God at the start of each day, before each meal and when saying your prayers before bed. Do it methodically and systematically. Do not forget. / Wisdom cries out in the streets, and no man regards it. / Give the dead children your heart. Give it to them so they can squeeze, twist, cut and chop it into pieces. Give it to them, and you'll see. / I'll do what I can, but only death can save you from life. / Jesus of the Garden, by your intercessions help me get over these bouts of dizziness and nerves. / They're not meant to be read by children. / Mask, do you know me? / Sex for affection, spit for tears. / Piruri, pirururiii. Castraaaaator! / Andrés Serrer received the chain, didn't believe it and threw it away in disgust. Nine days later his wife, who was carrying their child, died. / There are numerous situations in the day that offer you the opportunity to insult his name. It could be said that any opportunity is good to shit on God. / Spit it out, spit it out of your mouth. / Stop suffering, leave what you're doing and come running! / Why did you leave me for someone better-looking, kinder, more affectionate and more intelligent? I can't understand it. Why? / *A desfrutar.* / Neuroses, depression, stress, sexual dysfunction, tel. 592112, Dr Carmen Castiñeiras. / If you say any more ugly words, I'll wash your mouth out with soap.

(Whorish) Desire

Aaah, whore, the purity of the purest, basest desire. Ah, hooker, the essence of pure, abstract, animal desire. Ah, wench, love, the desire of the basest, most essential purity. That bitch's irresistible gesture, that trollop's obscene smile, is answered by a small, hot arabesque that stirs in my belly. Dammit, just let me get hold of you, let me grab your waist, you bitch. I shit on Christ, damn puta, those blouse-cellophaned tits make my chromosomes dance about, laughing hysterically at me. How I love you, slut. Darling. Horizontal love, little love. Go on, my precious, let me touch you. What pretty hair you have. I like the way it's so black. Did you dye it black or is that its natural colour? Pretty heart, sweet hustler. I really like you, love you, you know. I love you too much, more than I should. Go on, my love, stop hustling. Come with me. Be a hooker for my eyes only. Just for me.

Wait just a minute, the king of the Greeks wasn't Agamemnon. He was another general. The king of the Greeks was Priam. That was it, now I remember. I made a mistake. You see, the Greeks all have these similar names... Priam, that was it. He was a cousin of Agamemnon's, as you might have guessed.

There's also the adventures of Odysseus, but I haven't written about them yet.

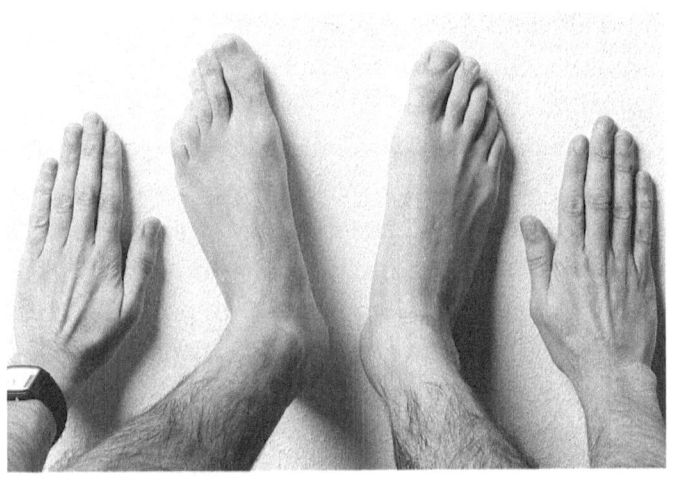

Driver

I'm a driver, driving my car, *conduzo o meu coche*, *conduzo o meu coche*, I head down the road, *a miña estrada*, zoom past, *conduzo o meu coche*, zoooom.

It's raining *na estrada*, raining hard *na estrada*, on the landscape as well, the wipers can't get rid of the water on the windscreen because *chove forte, forte, forte*, and I pass a hunched, barefooted old woman talking to herself, leading a donkey by a rope in the opposite direction, and I can't say what little patch of hell that woman with her wet head and keen gaze carries inside her head, nor do I want to know, so I pay attention to my driving, because I'm a driver, driving my car, the old woman is left behind, *conduzo o meu coche, conduzo o meu coche*.

Fourth Sorrowful Mystery

USURY AND CONSTIPATION, ASEPSIS AND STERILITY

That's why, when one dies, everything one has said, everything one has thought, all the pretty and ugly things that have gone through your head, go away. It's a shame really. There should be a kind of archive where the head or soul of each person could be kept. So many miracles are performed with all the technology there is, if they wanted, they could put a person's soul inside one of those little crumbs they call a chip, and all of them could be kept inside a warehouse. For example, take Pico Sacro, hollow it out and put all the chips with souls in there. Millions of chips. And then, when one dies, goes off into the potato field, along comes a relative of yours, your child or grandchild, wanting to know what this fellow was really like. You press a button on a computer, and the soul appears and can be heard talking. In that way, someone could really get to know an ancestor of theirs, and in that way we could also get to know ourselves better. Because there are lots of cases in which a trauma or a frustration, a way of being, comes from someone who lived before us and passed it down to us. Isn't that right? Positively, such things have been scientifically proven. This could be applied in so many ways. I wish, for example, I could get to know my own father. My real father, I mean. The one who made me inside my mother. The one who later married her, Xosé, well, he's also my father because he brought me up, but I mean the one who inserted the seed. I'm talking about Don Isidro Puga Fernández, a very famous doctor back then. Nowadays, nobody remembers him, of course. He was the father of Don Isidro Puga Pena, the professor and philosopher who went mad and was admitted to the sanatorium of Dr Deus Figueira, the nerve doctor. This philosopher lived many years in Lugo, before moving over here. He and I, well, I think we're brothers on our father's side. Isidro, our father, was already getting on when he made my mother pregnant, he must have been close to sixty and already had another son, Don Isidro, who must have been in his thirties, I reckon. So this gentleman, my brother, is thirty-something years older than me. He must have been a real bastard, that Don Isidro – our father, I mean – because he took advantage of my mother, she was just a girl and needed the work, she was a servant in his household. My mother never talked about it, I found out from my aunt Milucha, the one with the bar at the bus station. My mother was sick in bed, she used to get chest infections all the time, and so he went to see her, needless to say, he was a doctor, and she was a servant in his house. He went and made her a child. Made me, in effect. Men are like dogs. They're capable of fucking a pig if there's nothing else to hand. They're a bunch of pigs. There are all sorts. Being a man is like a sickness. That's the saddest part, one sometimes wonders about life, why the fuck did we come into the world? It's a hard one, that is. It's a hard question to ask. Especially if you're aware that you're in this world because of some bastard who took advantage of your mother. It's one thing to go with a man because you love him, quite another to abuse somebody, right, that's abuse. So I'm the result of this abuse that bastard inflicted on my mother. If you think about it, it's hard to think you're the result of some abuse. Life is a form of abuse, let me tell you, I'm not so young any more. Life is a struggle. He who doesn't drink blood dies of hunger. Not me, eh. I prefer to sit here quietly, not bothering anybody, it never even occurred to me to work or something. OK then, I worked a bit, I even spent a period in the Gran Sol, that's real work, days, weeks on end, hardly sleeping, chopping up bait, 'Catch some mackerel, lad!' they'd say, and I'd catch some mackerel. Pulling in the fish, pulling in the fish. Always wet, hardly sleeping. That was when I lost my hand, it got stuck in a machine that wound in the rope and, by the time I realized, it had gone, seen and not seen, Evaristo. Fodder for the sardines. That's a hard one, you betcha. A bunch of men enclosed, with not a woman in sight. Well, just one, this inflatable doll. That's a hard one. I've written about my experiences in a notebook. The thing is I don't know an editor. And besides, I'm pretty sure they'd prefer to publish someone who's more famous. I bet you if I turned up at one of those companies with my notebooks, they'd just laugh at me. I don't have any studies, you see. But what I write is worthy of consideration, not just because it's literature, but because it's written with my left hand, that makes it more worthy. It took a lot of work to learn how to write with my left hand, and it seems that the things one writes with one's left hand are somehow truer. Whether you like it or not, you have to think about them more slowly, it's as if you had to be more deliberate. Something that's been written more slowly and with the left hand carries more weight. More courage, because it's harder to do. I'm sure the things haven't been written properly, as if a person with studies had written them with his right hand. But there's a lot of philosophy and worldology in the stuff I've written. I may not have worked very much – a couple of years as a waiter, a couple of years in a chocolate factory, the odd occupation, working as an errand boy for a drugstore, that kind of thing. I may not have had much experience – I never got married and don't have children, and that kind of stuff – but, even though I don't have much experience, I see what other people get up to. And I learn. You see, there are some folk who get up to all kinds of stuff, but never learn. I see what people get up to, I see what they're doing, and I learn. I draw conclusions: this guy's doing well because he acted in such a way; that guy's not doing so well because he behaved in that way. I watch and learn. Should I ever want to be myself and do things, that day would be the tops. The tops. You see, I have a lot of worldology. A lot. The thing is the years go by and nobody's immune to years. Immune means you can't hurt it. You know what it's like with years and the passage of time, they wear you down. Time kills. Sex and time are illnesses, but time is worse, it can finish sex off. There are those who say they like killing time, but I just laugh, there's nobody that can kill time, it's time that kills you. Not even Christ could deal with time and, when his hour arrived, there was nothing he could do. The poor man called out to his father and said, 'Why hast thou forsaken me?' The other, not a dicky bird; when his hour arrived, that was it. Poor guy didn't know who the other was, but I'm fully acquainted with that old assassin. Hours kill, minutes as well. Not so much, but they kill. I've seen it, I'm not so young any more. I'll be thirty-five soon. No, not thirty-five, fifty-five. Or was it forty-five? Blast, I never remember, I'll have to talk to my mother. My memory's not so good. For some things. For others, my memory works extremely well. I know the lives of every Christ out there. Every Virgin Mary. In this little head of mine, there's room for the whole world. I'm not so dumb as people say, just because I don't work and don't have a family, just because I like to wet the old palate, a little Ribeiro wine if someone's paying, they think you're dumb. If you're not the way people want you to be, then you're an oddball, an idiot. They're a bunch of loonies. I'm not dumb at all. Besides, if I never worked, it's because I lost my hand, what do they think? I don't work, but I don't beg either, I don't need to, I may not be rich, but I've enough for a thimble of wine and a pack of smokes. Besides, I'm hardly going to go begging with a rubber hand, am I? People would think I was making fun of them. They think this whenever I introduce myself, 'My name is Nano, and this is my hand,' and hold out my hand. And besides, if Don Isidro the son, I mean Don Isidro Puga Pena... well, if this Don Isidro was a professor and philosopher, I think he even wrote some books... if this Don Isidro was a philosopher, not any more, he's in a bad way now, poor fellow, he was admitted to a psychiatric clinic, Dr Deus Figueira's, I think... Seems he went crazy. This guy who works at the clinic and is married to my sister-in-law told me Don Isidro had gouged out his eyes. That's terrible. That's tremendous, that is. My goodness, a person's head can get into a right muddle. We're really nothing at all. If your head turns against you, well, there's nothing worse than your head going all topsy-turvy. If you don't tell your member who's boss, that's bad enough. But if you lose your head, then you're reduced to nothing. Just some unruly flesh. You have to stay in control, always. That's what my father used to say. Not Don Isidro, no, not that bastard – I mean our father, sick Don Isidro's father and mine. The one who used to say you had to stay in control was the one who later married my mother, Xosé. He was a very good man. It was a shame he gave himself over to drink. Had I never found out he wasn't my real father, I'd have thought my taste for Ribeiro came from him. I only like wine, it has vitamins and carbohydrates. Look, take a proper look, if you look well, you can almost see the vitamins. I don't go in for spirits or any of that stuff. Just wine. But as I was saying... if Don Isidro the son was a philosopher, and we're brothers, then wouldn't some of the philosophy have rubbed off on me? Of course it would. I reckon. We even look a bit alike, I've noticed when walking past him in the street he has an aquiline nose like mine. His ears jut out a bit. Not the eyes, his eyes are blue, he has his mother's eyes, I've heard tell she was a piano teacher. But the intelligence must have been shared between us, I think. Anyway, they're rich, and I don't have anything to do with them. They've never had dealings with us, Don Isidro the doctor, the one who made me, as soon as my mother got pregnant, didn't want to know any more about the matter, and in the end he kicked her out. He offered her a few pennies, the bastard, but my mother wouldn't take them. She went back to the village, to the house of my grandparents, her parents, and raised me there until I was three, then came back to the city, I stayed until I was six and then came back as well. By that time, my mother had married this other guy, Xosé. I received a lot of affection and understanding from my mother's family. Considering the circumstances. From the other family, none at all. Children need to be loved, God dammit. Children need to be loved. Of course, it was much worse for my mother, she was only a girl, barely seventeen, I think. She never quite got over what the old man did. There are still times today when she starts shouting out at night that she's being attacked by a birdie. She dreams an eagle is attacking her. It's all because of what happened. It's obvious the eagle represents the old man. It was a trauma for her. And I don't know whether my own dreams don't have something to do with old Isidro. Perhaps the Bogeyman is the old man himself. It may sound unlikely, but it's not entirely implausible, I reckon he's sometimes so keen to attack people, boys and girls most of all, he takes the form of a person. I've seen him sometimes dressed up as a policeman, a castrator, blowing his whistle, a builder... Perhaps I am the Bogeyman's son. I'm just afraid he may catch me some day and kill me. That's my fear. Though, of course, it could just be a figment of my imagination. It's something I have to bear in mind, but the fear is real. I wouldn't mind dying so much if it served to free humanity of this ending. If my death helped in some way. Then people would say, 'Thanks to Nano for saving us.' But he may just finish me off, and it won't help in the slightest.

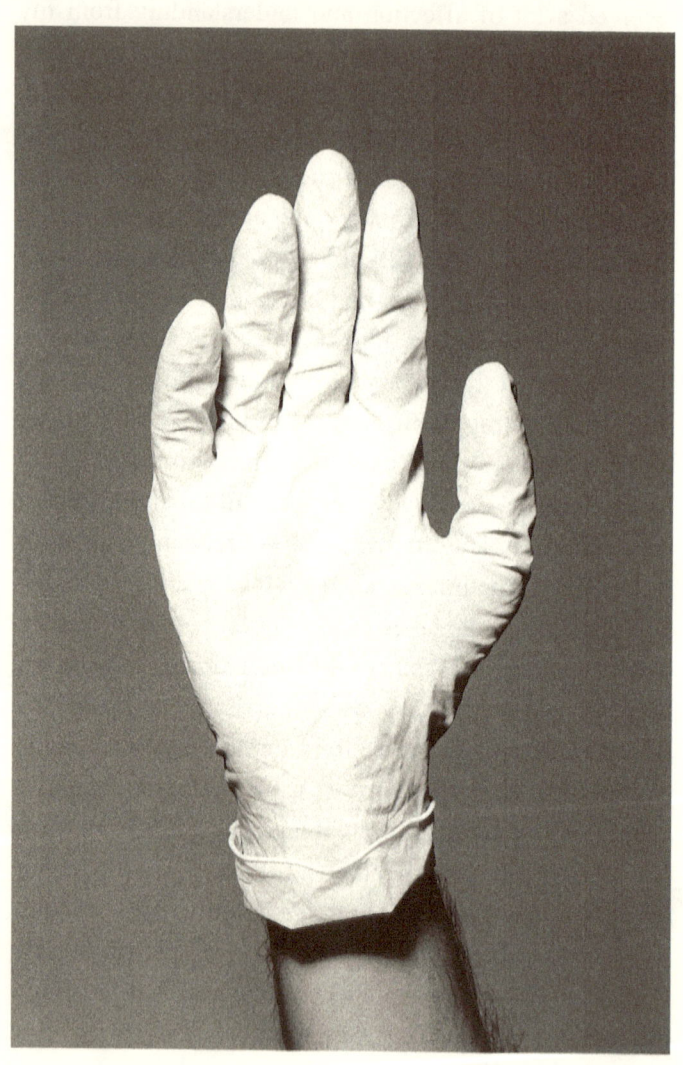

Wait There

Wait there, I'm coming. Let's see now, what's this little girl up to? You don't want me to catch you. Watch out, I'm coming. Don't run, I'm after you. What a little minx this girl is! What's this little bottom, what am I going to do with it? Ah, ah, ah, what's the little girl up to? What's she up to? Ah, I'm going to catch her, ah, I'm going to catch her. I'm going to catch this little trickster, this little minx. Ah, ah, ah. This little ant. Aumm, I'm going to eat her, I'm going to eat her. Aumm, aumm, I'm going to eat her little leg, I'm going to eat her little leg. Ah, here goes now. Shall I eat it? Shall I eat this podgy leg? No, I won't eat it. No, no, I'm not going to eat it, noooo. Little thing, pretty little thing. Who's my little girl, then, who? How I love her, I do. Little shrimp. Little imp. My rounded cabbage.

Artists

Is an artist melancholy, with slow but sad movements? His gaze passes over surfaces, faces and objects, not noticing anything or anyone, eaten up as he is by the sadness that devours him inside. A small, cold, but voracious fire that drains his energy for anything that isn't the affirmation of that tiny blaze inside him. His hair, his dishevelled locks, show this to be the case, and the flight of his cape demands silence of those that watch him pass.

Is an artist irate, does he give off a masterless desire for fury in his gestures? His eyes irradiate energy that is focused in a glance when he looks, just for a moment, and you glimpse the rage of radical rebellion and the glow of intimate nakednesses. Nothing can disturb the vision of that uninhabited landscape, devoid of the ashen colour contained in the pupils of his eyes. His face contorted in perpetual tension creates a field of solitude around him, and the thick worsted jacket shows anyone that draws near the rigour of his feeling and the severity of his behaviour.

Is an artist cynical, does he at a distance make a mockery of everything and everyone? His laughter, his mediocre, vulgar gestures designed to cloak from the gaze of the ignorant the undoubted glow encased in his chest that slides like a reptile to the attentive eye between vain words and mean gestures he severely, bitterly and ritually carries out. He is nourished by the admiration of a few capable of seeing the golden flush in his taunts, the pain in his laughter. The contempt and disgust as he purses his lips is a sign he tastes defeat before undertaking the struggle, and the raised eyebrow houses a glance that is definitely bitter, though it may appear cynical.

Ah, artists! Almost always martyrs, hardly ever heroes! They bang on metals at high temperatures, but can't get rid of the coldness in their bones. Move aside, the artists are coming! Don't look into their eyes, mere mortals! Ah, jeepers, they give me the creeps.

Machine

This is the 'machine of the round hole'. It would be more exact or scientific to call it 'of the circular hole', but the fact is it's called 'of the round hole', 'machine of the round hole'. That's the way things are, which are never, or almost never, as they should be.

It's more or less a white box, probably made of painted wood, though it could be made of tin or another metal painted white. It's about a metre high and has a circular lid about forty centimetres in diameter. The measurements are approximate. There's a chair in front of it.

A man arrives and sits on the chair facing the machine. He crosses his legs and gazes at the machine. Nothing, nothing happens. The seated man bangs the floor with the end of his foot, tap, tap. Nothing, still nothing happens. I couldn't say whether anything will happen. The way things are... The seated man shuffles in his seat, seems to be getting bored. Now, finally, he fiddles with the round, or rather circular, lid, looks as if he's going to take it off. Yes, he's taken it off. He places the lid on top very carefully and waits. Nothing, nothing happens or is seen. It looks empty, it's completely dark inside. The man approaches the hole and peers in. Ooh, what a fright. The man quickly steps back, from the hole appear two hands and a foot that shake and wriggle about. The man standing there appears annoyed that the machine has frightened him. Yes, he's annoyed. He takes the lid and uses it to castigate the hands and feet, which slowly withdraw inside. He closes the lid. He gives the machine a bad-tempered stare. A moan seems to emanate from the machine, yes, it's a moan like the whimper of a dog or some such animal. The man gives the machine a kick, and it shuts up. Nothing can be heard now, the man stands there, gazing at the machine. He's annoyed. Now the man leaves, stops, turns to look at the machine, leaves. Leaves for good.

Would you look at that! The machine of the round hole gave the man that sat in front of it a real fright. And he got really annoyed. Though it made for a pitiable object when it started moaning like that. It sounded as if it were suffering. There's no telling with such things. My goodness, you never can tell. Now a dog is coming. Well, blow me down! The dog's peeing on the machine! I blame the owners for not keeping their dogs on a leash.

(From Nano's notebook *Dictionary of Things and Inventions I Invented*)

Paraplegia

I stopped playing – you carry on, I can't any more – and went to sit down, still breathless, next to Nito so I could talk to him and keep him company. Nito was smiling as always in his wheelchair. You get tired? I got tired, I can hardly breathe. I took off one shoe and rubbed the sweaty sock, those shoes were a bit tight. Nito gazed at my hands massaging my foot and carried on smiling. I wish I could do what you're doing, he said. He carried on gazing at my foot. I let my hands go limp and remained motionless, watching my friends, who carried on playing and yelling. But you can take your foot in your hands, I said and looked at him. He carried on smiling under his small, blond moustache. Yes, but my feet can't feel anything when they're being massaged. I went back to gently massaging my sweaty sock. It had a hole in the end, which revealed part of my nail. What can you do then? I don't know, he carried on smiling. You can do other things, I said in order to say something. What kind of things? he asked, still smiling. Well, I don't know, he gazed at me with a smile. I stood up and slapped him first on one side, then on the other, then I grabbed the chair and lifted it in the air and threw him out. He groaned on the ground, lifted his hand to the blood coming out of his mouth. Then he looked at me and smiled. I left, holding my shoe.

When I looked back, my friends were standing around him, helping him back into the chair and shouting at me in annoyance. God dammit.

To the Exact Degree

I open the door to the apartment with the usual, exact noises. Hang on, the door just squeaked. Yes, it was a squeak. I turn it again, yes, the door is creaking. Tomorrow I'll have to get the cleaner to spray some oil on the hinges. The dog and cat come to greet me with diligence. Good, as it should be. As every day. Hello, have you behaved yourselves? I know full well you've behaved yourselves. I remove my coat and scarf and hang them on their hook. Now my jacket. What a pleasant atmosphere, air that is clean, warm and humid to the exact degree. Air that carries a hint of cleaning and clothes that have been ironed and treated with softener and scent diffuser. I take a deep breath to forget the stench of filth in the elevator. All sorts use that lift.

I switch on the halogen lamp, which spreads over the functional, clean, smooth, matt-finished furniture.

All right, all right, out of the way. Don't rub against my legs, you know I don't like it. I don't want to smell of cat and dog and have other cats and dogs sniffing all over me. OK then. I'll give your necks a stroke, I know you like it. Just a little. Don't tell me you're deprived of attention. There goes, each hand giving each neck a stroke. That's enough. Off you go, back to your corners. I said to your corners. That's right.

I turn on the tuner and the CD player. Sonata in G major for piano and violin, K. 379, by Mozart begins to play. First the piano. Now the violin joins in. I walk down the clean, sparkling corridor to the sound of the music and switch on the kitchen light. Good, good, the cleaner has put everything away. I never could remember the cleaner's name. How incredibly scatterbrained I was when it came to names. Unless it had to do with work, I was always forgetting people's names.

I open the fridge. Perfect, dinner ready in a pot. I take it out and put it in the microwave. The music reaches me. The dog and cat come in. Aha, you're hungry, you little imps. I open the door of the cupboard where I keep their food. I take out the packages of dog and cat food. Proteins, vitamins, fibres and minerals. Dinnertime, folks. I heap some food on to their plates, they come over slowly. Good nourishment. I put the packages away. I notice some fat on my hand, the cupboard handle must be a little dirty. Not properly clean. Tomorrow I'll have to leave a note for the cleaner. To clean it properly. Surfaces touched with hands should be cleaned at least once a week with cotton wool soaked in alcohol. That kills off the bacteria.

The dog and cat eat slowly from their plates. They still have water in their bowls. I'll have to change it before going to bed, I don't want them getting germs. There's no need to catch infections unnecessarily. I like things to be aseptic and sterilized as well, if at all possible. Everybody would save themselves a lot of trouble and disease if they just followed a few basic rules of hygiene and asepsis. The glaring gap in education is not instilling hygienic habits at an early age. It's all a question of routine.

The bell on the microwave goes off. Lalaralalaaa. I dish up the food. Take a thin glass and pour out a little red wine from the bottle in the fridge. Off to the sitting room. Lalaralalaaa.

The dog and cat follow me in. Now you're full you want to play, eh? I open the lacquered wooden box on the shelf and take out the plastic mouse and bone. Playtime. Stop right there, no jumping, settle down. What do polite animals do? What? That's it. Now you can have them, the mouse for you and the bone for you. Off you go, play while I'm eating. That's it, make the most of it.

I can hear noises in the flat next door, that fat woman shouting with her kids. I turn up the volume, let the sound of the piano and violin enfold me. The younger kid always has bleary eyes and a runny nose. It must be from some kind of infection. Or just from crying, he's always crying. Either him or his sister, the one with holes in her teeth. That's from eating sweets. A completely nonsensical diet. Better concentrate on my food. And the music. The wine's a touch cold.

I've had enough. I shouldn't have eaten it all, there was too much sauce. Too many calories. Plus those in the wine. I'll have to tell the cleaner to cook with a little less sauce. Lalaralalaaa. Majestic. Aaah. Why not stretch out if I'm all alone? Aaah. You don't mind, do you, boys? It's not good to do this, it's impolite. Why does the body have need of so many things that are impolite? It's horrible when someone stretches out in public, it's extremely obnoxious. The person looks like a gorilla. He always tried not to do this. But nobody could see him now. I'm tired, I need to relax. Time for bed.

I stand up. Turn off the music. I want you to sleep now as well, OK? I see you understand. I don't want to hear a peep out of you two, your master is off to bed. I'll let you have the toys during the night, but no noise. Good night then. I switch off the light and head for the bedroom.

I switch on the light and take off my clothes until I'm in my vest and pants. I take my keys from my trouser pocket and open the door of the wardrobe, which is locked.

I gaze at the doll. All dressed and ready. Carefully take her out. She has the softness of human flesh. The softness of firm muscle, tense flesh. I squeeze her against me. How hard and appealing are those breasts against my chest. I bet there's not a single woman has tits as soft and hard as mine does.

Would you care to dance, madam? I hold her and dance, lalaralalaaa, over to the main light and switch it off. I switch on the bedside lamp. Humm, you do dance well. I haven't seen you before, are you from these parts?

Circles

Two men were walking. Two men were walking. Two men were walking. Two men were walking. Two men were walking. Two men were walking. A girl leaning out of the window. Two men were walking. A girl leaning out of the window. Two men were walking. A girl leaning out of the window. Two men were walking along a path. A girl leaning out of the window gazed into the distance. Two men were walking along a path. A girl leaning out of the window gazed into the distance. Two men were walking along a path. The sun had set, all that could be seen were shadows. A girl leaning out of the window gazed into the distance and thought she would like to marry a man from a big city and go and live there. Two men were walking along a path. The sun had set, all that could be seen were shadows. A girl leaning out of the window gazed into the distance and thought she would like to marry a man from a big city and go and live there. Two men were walking along a path, they had come from work and were wearily discussing their things. The sun had set, all that could be seen were shadows. A girl leaning out of the window gazed into the distance and thought she would like to marry a man from a big city and go and live there, she saw the two men approaching on the path and with a weary gesture went back inside. Two men were walking along a path, they had come from work and were wearily discussing their things as they drew near to the house with its lights on. The sun had set, all that could be seen were shadows, all that could be heard were the two walkers' distant voices and the song of the crickets.

Bricolage/Popular Mechanics

MATERIALS: a crowbar, an ice axe.

INSTRUCTIONS: choose a time when you are not at home, check there are no neighbours in the other apartments on the same floor, call at each apartment several times (if they answer, say you need a little salt or vinegar). Having checked there is no one, call the lift and leave the door open so it can't go up or down. Now quickly place the crowbar between the frame and the door on a level with the lock. Pull hard and forcefully, repeat a couple of times until the lock breaks. Enter without making any noise and pull the door to. Should you now appear by any chance, because you were asleep or in the toilet, do not hesitate, hit yourself on the head with the crowbar. If in effect you're not at home, start turning the rooms over. Start with the nearest, the guest room, open the chest of drawers and scatter everything over the floor, then the wardrobe, pull off the sheets, blankets, throw them on top of the bed. There's no money or anything of value, leave everything in a mess and go out. Now go to your bedroom, open the bedside table, throw everything on the bed, take the two 5,000-peseta notes, rummage through the rest of your stuff, grab the wristwatch Nati gave you and the leather wallet you never use, take them with you. Don't forget to open the wardrobe as well and scatter your clothes on the floor.

Now quickly head to the living room and, using the ice axe, smash the colour TV screen (don't forget to unplug it first). To round things off, smash the mirrors in the bathroom and hallway. Now grab one of the plastic bags from the shop next door, which you keep under the sink, and place the tools inside. Leave at once. Close the lift door and go down the stairs.

Walk normally to a dustbin and place the bag, money, wristwatch and wallet inside. That's it. Now buy the paper at the kiosk and head calmly home while reading it. Take the lift up.

Open the door of the lift in a natural way, it's important to do this naturally, and search for your front-door keys, 'hey, what's this? The door's already open.' Stand stock-still, 'is there somebody in the apartment? I didn't give anybody the key.' Go closer, there are signs the door has been forced open. Turn cold. 'Somebody's been in my house.'

Push the door gently, are they still inside? Enter slowly, you can't hear a thing, the door of the guest room is open, everything in a mess, the violence turns your stomach, enter slowly, nobody there. Go out and continue, careful behind the doors, the kitchen door is ajar, push it open, nobody there, go in. It's empty. In the bathroom, the mirror is broken, bastards. How about the living room and bedroom? In the living room, the TV screen has been smashed, lowlife, you feel like crying, God dammit, you hadn't even finished paying it off. Go to the bedroom, careful now, they could be waiting for you, grab a knife from the kitchen. Kick the door open, everything in a mess, drawers all over the place, all your things, photos, letters, scattered on the floor. Nobody. Little bastards. Sons of bitches. Rummage through your things, they've taken the money, 10,000. And Nati's watch. Bastards, start picking up the photos, the wallet is missing. Sit down on the bed. What a shitty thing to happen, it feels as if they're still in the house, everything pillaged and plundered. It feels as if it's not your house any more. You can barely breathe, better go and get some fresh air. How awful.

(From *Manual of Self-Harm* by A. HIGGINS)

Why

He silenced the alarm clock's annoying buzz. Time to get up. Better get out of bed, otherwise he'd carry on sleeping. He'd be late for work. His nose was dry from the heating. And his head hurt. Up you get.

Sitting on the bed, with his head in his hands, he thought about the bad taste in his mouth. He didn't have decay in any dental fixture, he'd been to the dentist for a check-up not two months earlier. He brushed his teeth four times a day, carried his folding toothbrush around with him in his jacket pocket. His toothpaste was the best and most expensive, and yet he had a bad taste in his mouth. He took care over his dentures and followed a rational diet, and yet he had a bad taste in his mouth. Halitosis. He could chew sugar-free gum to get rid of the bad smell, but that wouldn't get rid of the halitosis. He was clean and careful, it was his body, his stomach, that let him down. Why were we made of damp intestines. Intestines full of liquids and residues in a state of decay. To stop us being perfect.

He held out his arm and pulled the cord of the blinds. The blinds went up a little to reveal a greyish morning. Shocking weather. The doll lay motionless in the square of morning light. He pushed it aside with his foot, he didn't want somebody in another building seeing it. The doll was always the same. She didn't have bad smells, she didn't sweat, she didn't lose her composure. She was definitely perfect. She didn't get tired. Always ready.

He was tired. He always slept for eight and a half hours, but got out of bed feeling tired, battered. He didn't sleep well. He passed his hands over his stubble, how quickly it grew and how hard it was. A day's growth gave him an untidy appearance. It didn't matter if he was clean and showered, he still looked unkempt. Each and every morning, he had to fight this dishevelled look. With those eye bags he had when he got up. What a disaster, he preferred not to see himself in the mirror until he'd had breakfast, showered and shaved. He was just glad nobody else could see him in the morning. He couldn't have endured somebody else seeing him this tired and dirty, sitting on the bed. He didn't want anybody seeing him there in his pyjama bottoms soiled with dried semen, his stubble and dishevelled hair, sitting there without any energy on the edge of his unmade bed. He felt like lowering the blinds and getting back into bed.

His clothes were waiting for him to get dressed. His thermal vest lay crumpled on the floor. All his vests had to be thermal, otherwise he would get cold when wearing a shirt, but then they made him sweat like a pig under his armpits. He had a washbag in the drawer of his desk at work with a deodorant stick, but was still afraid of somebody finding him smelly in the afternoon if they got too close. He never got too close, but there were those who didn't know how to keep their distance.

The silk shirt would do for another day. It had been clean on the day before, you could use them for two days without having body odour. Body odour was the enemy, without your realizing, everything you touched became impregnated with the smell. Our bodies were like machines that corrupted our surroundings, giving off odours and bacteria. The Adolfo Domínguez silk tie looked a little shabby around the knot, but it wasn't that obvious and this was his favourite. His trousers had been perfectly positioned so they wouldn't lose their crease, these Armani suits kept their creases very well. In that suit and those shoes, he looked a little taller. Thanks to the raised insoles he put inside his shoes. Why hadn't he been born taller and more handsome. How humiliating if somebody found out. If somebody checked his shoes and saw him sitting there, all tired and dirty, with bags under his eyes. They'd all laugh at him. They'd all know he was nothing more than an ugly, smelly animal.

How odious was existence. Why couldn't we be the way we liked. Why did our bodies and instincts get in the way to prevent purity and perfection. You had to work every day to make it happen, to put on a pretence, but, come nightfall, everything fell by the wayside. It was like this every day. It was always like this. Work, work, work. He still had to clean and sterilize the doll before putting her away. And write a note to the cleaner, telling her to hoover the carpet more carefully, she always left marks. He had to get a move on if he didn't want to be late.

He heard the cat and dog's discreet footsteps outside in the corridor.

The Scene of the Crime

It is very true that one always returns to the scene of the crime. In this way, where there has been a death, the presence of evil remains unless it is exorcized. This is why murderers go back to the scene of their infamies, the hard-hearted savour their vile acts once again. Those with weaker or more sensitive hearts vainly attempt to exorcize the crime and lament the spilt blood.

All we criminals, all we adults on reaching old age, return to the scene of the crime. Return to childhood. Uselessly but obsessively, we visit the environs of childhood and puberty, but lack the strength to open locked doors. And even if we could open them, what would we find? The crimes committed against us, the crime we committed against ourselves. We would find Horror. And who could look Horror in the face?

That is why my memory looks carefully about, scrutinizing each detail of this place. And yet, while it wants to know, it also deceives itself, and me along with it. I cannot trust it, it lies. I should take some medicine, we are chemistry and in chemistry should seek what we lack.

That something we have always lacked and noticed. I'm talking about the wound. I'm talking about the hurt, the flaw, the lack, the flaw, the stump, the pus, the missing arm, the illness, the lame leg, the disquiet, the high blood pressure, the blocked artery, the swollen prostate, the hysterectomy, the castration, the swollen lymph node, the inflammation, the loss of hair, the passage of time. All we have is chemistry against Death of a thousand faces. Foul Gorgon.

(Manuscripts of ISIDRO PUGA PENA)

Come Back with the Meat

Dressed in an old, dirty, frayed shirt of uncertain colour, with grey, greasy locks, five days' worth of stubble and a potent smell, he sits in front of a dirty table with the remains of dinner. He looks as if he's in pain and holds a hand against his cheek. He rocks to and fro on the stool he is sitting on and, from time to time, lets out an animal groan. Through one window enters a weak, mournful light and a scene absolutely overcast by a merciless, wind-driven deluge. The room is full of rubble and old, rusty, dust-covered junk.

Through one door staggers an animal that looks like a dog coated in tangled locks with mangy bald patches. Through the hair on its head appear two red dots lost in the depths of its eye sockets. From its mouth flicks a reptilian tongue accompanied by a noise like the crack of a whip. It passes next to the seated man. When he sees it, he gives it a kick. The animal jumps to one side with a cry that is almost human, then sticks out its threatening tongue. Finally it collapses beneath the clarity of the window.

Through the selfsame door enters a fat woman with bright, coloured cheeks. She's wearing a grey headscarf and a dress with an apron that is the same dirty grey colour. She's smiling and holding a bowl in one hand and a piece of mouldy bread in the other. She places the bread and bowl, spilling something on the table, in front of the seated man.

'Come on, you bastard. Have your breakfast and stop faffing about. What kind of Baddie do you think you are? Pervert.'

'I just wish you had toothache like mine, you slut. That would make me laugh,' groans the Baddie, still with his hand on his cheek.

'Come on then, open your mouth, you jerk.'

The other opens his mouth, revealing a pair of enormous, black, gaping jaws with large, yellow, uneven canines in the front and large, black molars at the back. He waggles a huge, damp, wrinkled, red tongue and lets out a threatening 'aaaaaahh', which he sustains like the drone of a malignant bagpipe.

The woman pretends to take a look, but in the meantime produces a lizard from her apron pocket and quickly stuffs it in his mouth. The woman moves away, laughing; the Baddie spits out the lizard, roars and suddenly in his hand wields an enormous knife he points at the woman. The animal jumps after the lizard and swallows it whole, its tail disappearing down one side of the animal's mouth. The woman laughs, covering her mouth with one hand and holding her belly with the other. The animal goes back to lying down. The Baddie puts the knife in the sheath hanging from his belt and shakes his fist at the woman.

'I don't want any of your mucking around in the morning, damned woman!'

The woman stops laughing, turns serious and kicks the animal, which gets up and quickly leaves the room with a moan.

'What? What you got for them today?' asks the woman, standing in the light of the window.

The man noisily slurps the muddy soup in the bowl,

his head on one side in an attempt to prevent the liquid coming into contact with his damaged tooth. He carefully bites off a bit of bread and talks with his mouth full:

'Auve flot shtlyap...'

'You what, turtlehead?'

The Baddie swallows what's in his mouth.

'I've got a trap prepared for them, God dammit!'

'Yeah, right. You put a bomb on the plane that was supposed to finish them off, but the Boy and that fucking Girl jumped out with a parachute and didn't even scratch themselves. You can't do anything properly, you useless lump.'

'I suppose you think you could do better, hairy loaf.'

'If there were bad girls instead of bad guys, don't you reckon we'd do better than you wasters? I'd have those two for my breakfast.'

The Baddie finishes what's in the bowl, and the liquid runs down the sides of his mouth. He smashes the bowl on the floor and does a burp. A turnip leaf dangles from his chin.

'You can stop with your feminist crap because I've had enough of that, you slut. They won't get past today. I have a nice little trap prepared for them on the path in the forest that leads to the treasure. A ditch full of nice, pointy stakes. When they walk along the path, wham! What? You reckon it will work? Ha, ha, ha.'

The woman laughs along with him. The Baddie puts his hand back on his cheek with a pained expression. The woman grabs a damp cloak from a hook on the wall and gives it to him.

'Come on then, stop messing around. Take your axe and get the hell out of here. I wouldn't want you to miss them. Come on, slughead.'

The Baddie gets up and puts on the cloak. He grabs an enormous axe from the corner of the room.

'Remember to dip the axe in a pool of filthy water before you hit them, so their wounds get nice and infected,' says the woman as she buttons up the cloak. 'And take your hat with you, you're going to catch a cold, numbskull. When you arrive, you always look a mess.' She removes the hat from another hook on the wall and gives it to him.

'Shut the fuck up. I'll do what the hell I like. I just hope they don't die at once, so I can watch them suffer.'

'I wish I could come with you. But with that hairy cow about to give birth... If you see it's getting dark and they still haven't died, then finish them off with the axe and come back home. I don't want you enjoying yourself too much and getting a head cold. You heard me, you dolt? Come on, get to work!'

They move to the threshold of the house. The door consists of two superimposed leaves; the upper one is open and reveals the flood.

'What pisses me off is that, even in this downpour, the mascara on that sluttish Girl's face isn't going to run. Some people have all the luck,' says the woman resentfully. She blows her nose with her hand and flings the snot into the rain.

'I'll make sure their luck doesn't hold for much longer,' says the man in a hoarse, threatening tone.

She sticks her hand on his crotch and grabs his genitals.

'Swear by this little fellow that you'll hurt them. Swear to me!'

'I swear I'll make them twist and groan. I swear I'll make them shout and bleed. I swear I'll cause them permanent damage and cripple them. I swear I'll do them in. And if I can, and they're still alive, I swear I'll rape the little bitch before she dies and cut off his little tommy. I swear it.'

The woman's open eyes sparkle with childish, dreamy joy.

'That's my boy. That's my Baddie. Off you go now.' She pats him on the back and pushes him outside.

Under the rain, he bares his teeth and says:

'I'll bring you their hearts and a bit of lean meat so you can cook them in a pie!'

'Get off with you, you bastard. And come back with the meat. I'll be waiting with my skirts up. Off with you!'

He grunts in satisfaction, dripping water as he heads along the road to the forest.

'Take care neither of those little runts does you any harm!' shouts the woman from the door, but the figure marching along with the axe over his shoulder doesn't hear.

The animal goes up to the woman. She kicks it, and the animal runs back inside. She closes the lower leaf of the door and mutters:

'What a day for work! I bet he comes back with a wound or cold.'

Shame

Have a sense of shame, keep your end up, never give in to emotion, hold the bridle of your muscles and never allow the maxillary to hang or the orbicular to relax, that loss of control for a moment, just a moment, will permit the sternocleidomastoid and lumbars to follow in fatal, irreversible sequence. You will be lost. A man who relaxes a gesture once relaxes it every time. Shame. Rigour. Rigour and discipline. Don't you pee standing up? Masculine shame is what makes us different and superior, and what is masculine shame if not the facial and bodily muscles on a state of alert before an emotion that could crumple like an old cloth the serenity authority and valour you've set yourselves, maintaining your purpose is valour, preventing that tear is serenity, remaining impassive is authority, don't lose your sense of shame, let other, feminine, unruly creatures weep moan lament and mourn observe from the height of verticality the bodies reduced to animals twisting beside themselves and complaining, that is the distance between you and her and don't forget the higher you look the greater the distance will be. Where is valour if not in withstanding the impact of vile sentiment against you in seizing it with cold determination and in wringing its neck with precision cracking the tiny bones beneath its soft skin wrung by your fierce fingers? Where if not in flinging that ridiculous and inert body that wanted to move you lower your guard into the attic with other old objects deceased and mutilated sentiments? Don't you pee standing up? You don't shit standing up because you don't want to. God dammit, are there or are there not balls? If there are balls then go and shit on everybody, shit standing up from now on. And I don't want to hear a sound, not a sound, if anyone complains I'll give him a kick in the balls he'll never forget, I don't know if that's clear if I have expressed myself well enough, because if it's clear then it is but if it isn't I'd like to see the prick with a pair of balls to tell me, a man without balls is nothing not a man, let the man with a pair of balls with a pair of testiculars come and tell me so himself, I'll cut them off, but there aren't any balls and you're lucky because if there were I'd play a game of ping-pong with them, you're just a bunch of faggots shirt lifters is what you are and I don't like that kind of stuff I'm a man and I don't like someone ramming my behind you do you've still got one cock in your mouths and another in your rears, so don't come ranging my rump don't come ruffling my feathers you're just a bunch of marys but I'll do what I can to turn you into men. I want men and nothing other than men, shame, valour and discipline and if anyone thinks he has something to say let him come and suck on it. I don't know if that's clear. Is that clear?

(From the manual *Make Yourself a Man* by L. Lewis Jones)

One Doesn't Know Why One Opens One's Mouth

He said shame and discipline and he was right, trouble is he gets very nervous and sometimes goes over the top loses control and then doesn't know what he's saying. Don't pay attention to some of the things he comes out with. He doesn't think, he doesn't stop to think. They just come out. You can see what he's like, he's just a loafer. The important thing is what he meant to say, something we men should always have in mind, what's generally referred to as 'keeping one's end up'. So keeping one's end up is important, more important than you might think. Above all not giving in to sentimental effusions. No going soft, no spells of affection, no dampness in the eyes, no snotty noses. It's highly undesirable for a man, a real man, to linger over sentiments, to squander emotions. Because that's what it is, squandering emotions. Control, control and holding back emotions. An iron will... not an iron will, I mean a firm, steady will. A will that's in control. No authoritarianism, no, just a necessary healthy dose of will. Authoritarianism of the will. That's it, will and self-control should know no limits in their domain. Well, the odd limit, as with everything. But just a few, reduced limits, because if you start limiting everything then it'll all go to the dogs. If this one starts crying and that one is depressed then we've really fucked up. In short, what he meant to say is that you shouldn't pussyfoot around a man not only has to be a man he has to look like one. What do you have to do to look like a man? What kind of fucking question is that? If you don't know what to do to look like a man at this stage in the game then we may as well turn off the lights and get the hell out of here. No, I reckon the other was right to get angry with you. I'm only surprised he didn't bash your faces in because I'm starting to feel like I could really ram something down your behinds. What the fuck is this? I don't know why I even bothered to open my mouth. What the fuck!

(From the manual of practical exercises *How?* by J. J. JAMES, a companion to the manual *Make Yourself a Man* by L. LEWIS JONES)

Nostalgia

His daughter is on his lap, in his arms, the two of them sitting on the sofa, he rocks her as in a slow dance. Amália Rodrigues is singing a fado on the CD player. On the television they're showing the images of a video without sound, the travels and performances of a rock band, thousands and thousands of fans jumping and moving their arms in silence. The girl seems to have got over her fever and is now playing at sucking a spoon. In the window a flock of birds opens out, disintegrates, fades into the afternoon light. And he wonders how long it will take for sadness to appear or whether it's that melancholy that's been lurking about.

Noises in the House

Right now I thought I saw someone peering out of a window of the house. But then they disappeared, perhaps I thought so, but there wasn't. Perhaps there's nobody at home. Perhaps it was just a figment of my imagination. But I really did think so. I often look up at the windows and think I've seen a shadow flit by. One day, I'll have to go and knock at the door to see if there's still someone living there.

But I have quite enough, what with looking after the garden, it's so big. He used to be able to look after it better, but the weeds seemed to have become more abundant, he just couldn't get rid of them. It was as if they wanted to devour the garden and the house. Or perhaps he just didn't have enough strength, what with the passing of the years. The bushes he'd planted had been lost a long time ago, and all that was left were weeds. However hard he struggled with them, they carried on growing and were already his height.

He remembered when he tended the garden well, and guests would come to some of the parties that were held in the house and gaze at the garden in admiration and envy. He used to feel very proud. But now. That said, there hadn't been a party in the house for many years. It had gradually ceased to be inhabited, with fewer people in it. Perhaps there was still somebody living there. Sometimes he thought he saw a shadow flitting past a window. Just now, for instance.

One day, he would have to go to the door and knock. Who knows? There might still be somebody at home.

Dear Model

'Wait, I'm going to take a photo of you in that new dress. Sit down on the fountain. That's it. Now, look over here. No, not like that. Don't pull a face.'

'What kind of face?'

'The one you have now. With that gesture around your mouth.'

'What gesture?'

'Nothing, just forget it. You adopted a gesture of disgust.'

'Are you an idiot? It's my usual expression. My mouth is always like that. You didn't mind it so much last night.'

'All right, forgive me. Don't pay any attention. Come on then, let's see, put your hand in the water.'

'No, I'm not in the mood for photos any more.'

'Oh, don't get like that. It was just me being stupid. Come on, sit on the side of the fountain for a moment, you look great.'

'No, I don't want to be here any more.'

'Oh, come on, darling. I've said I was sorry. What more do you want? Let me take a photo. Come on, it won't take long.'

'All right, but finish quickly.'

'That's my girl.'

'How's my mouth?'

'Fine. But try not to appear so serious, you look as if you're going to headbutt somebody. And don't let your hand droop like that, it looks pretentious. Lay it on the stone.'

'What's wrong with my hand? What did it ever do to you? You're an idiot, you know, you can go to hell. I've had quite enough. First you ask me to pose, and then you're not satisfied.'

'Oh, don't get like that. All I did was ask you to move your hand.'

'No, you didn't. You said it looked pretentious. It seems the only thing you want to do is humiliate me. Well, you can go jump in a lake. Get Rita to pose for you, or your mother, she knows how to wipe off your dribble.'

'All right then, I'm sorry.'

'Uh-uh, that's quite enough.'

'It doesn't matter, we'll do the photos some other day.'

'No, we won't. If you want to practise your hobby, you can pay for a model who's prepared to put up with you.'

'All right, all right. It's over. I didn't mean to bother you, please forgive me. It's all in the past. That said, you do have a quick temper.'

'No, it isn't in the past. I don't know what it is when you take photographs, but you look at me differently. What's the matter, don't you like me? Well, I haven't changed.'

'All right then, don't worry, I won't take another photo of you.'

'Not one. I don't want you looking at me like that.'

A Son's Work

The most difficult part was done. He switched on the bathroom light with his elbow so he wouldn't get it smeared with blood. He went in and looked at himself in the mirror. He had bloody hands and red stains on his face.

He turned on the tap and left the mark of his besmirched fingers on the stainless steel. A drop that was almost black fell into the basin. He placed his hands under the stream of water and let it cascade, first on one, then on the other. His hands felt dead, they wanted to rest, to be still, not to have to work. The worst part had been tearing out his heart, that had led to a lot of blood. It was in the kitchen, on top of the chopping board. He'd always liked a bit of veal heart, he'd always asked for some from the butcher's ('Tell them it's for me, they'll put it aside', 'Yes, father'). It contained the calf's soul, he used to say, that was why it had such a strong taste. Now he would eat the other's soul. His black soul.

In the end, he started rubbing one hand against the other, scrubbing around his fingernails. It seemed the blood wanted to go inside him, not to leave. He formed a pool with his clean hands and lifted it to his face. The freshness of the water was comforting. He put more water on his face and let his damp fingers rub his eyes, slowly.

His eyes hurt deep inside, they must have been wide open. Or been damaged by what they'd seen. By what he'd made them see. He raised his wet face and gazed at it glistening in the mirror. In that hate-filled look, he discovered the other's look. It was the other's look. His own look was the one the other had had for the last time. When the other had looked at him with hate, only with hate. Not with fear, he didn't really think he was going to kill him. He thought he wouldn't dare. He wouldn't dare to kill his own father.

But that look, those eyes, belonged to the other. He'd always thought he took after his mother. He was the spitting image of his mother. But those fierce, bulging eyes were his father's. How come he hadn't noticed before? And the Adam's apple, the Adam's apple bobbing up and down in his throat, that was also his father's. He was taking after his father more and more. He passed his damp hands over his face. Looked at himself in the mirror through splayed fingers.

Machine

This machine is called 'for nothing'. That's it, 'machine for nothing'. I'm not quite sure what it's for. It looks like a white bucket, but is full of wheels, levers, keys, cranks... There it is, like a sitting-room harp in the dark corner, waiting for a hand to set it in motion.

There goes the errand boy. He looks at the machine. Puts down his handcart and cleans his hands on the nankeen apron, which is fairly dirty. He slowly approaches the machine and examines it all over. He presses a button, and a little red light goes on. He waits for a moment, but nothing, nothing else happens. So now he pulls a lever on one side. Nothing, nothing happens. He pulls it again, but nothing happens. He wipes his hands on the apron and stares at the machine in concentration. He tries turning the crank. The crank is resistant. He has to make a real effort, it's difficult, but finally the crank moves. Nothing happens. He carries on turning the crank until he gets tired. His face is congested, he wipes his hands on the apron and spits to one side. He presses another button, another red light goes on. He switches it off. He switches off the other light he turned on earlier. He spits in the same direction he spat in before, goes over to his handcart without taking his eyes off the machine, lifts the handcart and leaves with a puzzled look. It's hardly surprising. If it doesn't work after he's pressed and turned all those buttons and levers, then goodness knows how it will work. A machine that doesn't work, that's some kind of invention. There's no doubting it doesn't work, the errand boy has had a go at everything.

It's a wonder, some invention. People invent things because they can't stand still. It makes you wonder.

(From Nano's notebook *Dictionary of Things and Inventions I Invented*)

Driver

I'm a driver, you know, driving my car, *conduzo o meu coche, conduzo o meu coche, cariño*, I head down the road, *a miña estrada*, my journey, *a miña viaxe*, and zoom past, *nena, conduzo o meu coche*, zoooooom.

There's fog on the road, *brétema na estrada*, a thick fog that makes it difficult to see the lights of the other cars, it's almost night and driving is tiring, it would be good to get home, *á casa*, home, sweet home, switch on the light, the heater, sit on the sofa, read the paper, listen to music on the radio, *na radio*, but I have no home, no sofa, the only dealings I have are with the cats and dogs I run over, they lie on the road because I'm a driver, driving my car, *conduzo o meu coche, conduzo o meu coche*.

Fifth Sorrowful Mystery

THE BOGEYMAN'S WORK

No, writing isn't just anything. It's not as easy as people think. That's why I haven't plucked up the courage to publish everything I've written in a book. One day, I may pluck up the courage, if I get a bit of money together, if I win the lottery or something like that, then I'll go to the printer's and say, 'Make me a book.' The title I'd give it would be *Hitting Hard* because, if I ever brought out a book, then I'd say everything there is to say about life. Or else I'd call it *Autopsy*, which is what they do to you when you die in an accident or unfortunate circumstances. In an autopsy, they open you up and look inside and so find out everything about you scientifically. Well, not exactly everything, but almost. So in my book I'd say everything there is to say, as if it were an autopsy. Life as it is. Exactly as it is. A chaotic, nonsensical hodgepodge of voices and things, and I'd use the opportunity to include everything I've written in the book. Also, everything I've ever cut out, you see, whenever I come across a story I like in a book or article, well, I go and cut it out and keep it. So I'd put those things in as well. Photos even. I used to like to paint but, now I'm missing a hand, well, I sometimes hook up with a friend of mine who's a photographer and we take some photos. I might even call it *Tick-Tock*, now that's a real bummer, the passage of time. That's the number one bummer. Or else I'd call it *Cry, Baby, Cry*, because of all that business with children. Then, even if I did die at the hands of the Bogeyman, if I could just let humanity know first, humanity would be grateful and would read or say prayers from my book. As if it were a gospel or a rosary. Writing is tough, that's why you have to have a lot of worldology, you have to have observed life a lot and, above all, to have learned from it, which is something people don't do. If you know how to learn, which is the difficult part, then life can teach you a lot. A lot. Positively. Well then, I'd get down to writing seriously. I sometimes feel like it, after all, instead of talking non-stop, spending all this time pondering my things, better to put them down in words. That may also be a way of killing the words off, or at least of wielding control over them. Of instilling a bit of discipline. As my father used to say, Xosé, the one who died, the one who married my mother, well, he used to say, 'You have to stay in control, Nano.' He didn't stay in control very much, because of his drinking problem, the more he drank and swayed from side to side, the more he would say, 'You have to stay in control.' He was a good man, if we take away the drinking bouts. When he was drunk, he wasn't in control, he didn't know who we were, he used to call me 'Saviour'. He'd start off in that direction. I'm not even sure how he used to get home, it must have been the smell, like a dog, if you'll pardon the comparison. Well, I think writing is a way of controlling words. Words, if you let them, are stronger than you. You bet they are. If you stop and let them out, they start rushing through your head, coming and going, faster and faster, until they drive you crazy. If you let them out, they seize power. You see, they're very powerful. Sometimes I'm afraid when I see more and more words rushing through my head, I feel I'm going to go crazy. I'm afraid I'll choke on the words, I'll suffocate. Or my head will burst. Bang! And words will be scattered everywhere. A sort of contamination. You know what contamination is, it's when something is turned into a mess, well, the same thing, but with words. When it gets like that and I can't stand it any more, I start banging my fists against a wall. That way, my knuckles start to hurt and my head is taken up with something else, with the pain, it focuses on one thing only. That's how I get the words to stop driving me crazy. There may be other methods, of course, but this one works for me. I know it sounds a bit brutal, but it's quite scientific. In as far as it goes. To a greater or lesser degree. I use a similar method for toothache, now that's a terrible pain. So what I do is bang my head against the wall. It's not necessary to spill blood, you just have to hit it slowly, so you get a bruise or something. A bump. When my missing hand starts hurting – my phantom hand, that is – when it starts itching, now that's a real suffering, your hand is itching, you can feel it itching, but you can't scratch what isn't there, you can't give yourself any relief. That, my friends, is the worst thing that can happen to you. When that happens, what I do is I go to the gas stove, turn on the flame and stick my finger in the flame. It's better if it's a finger you don't use so much, your little finger, for instance. I burn it a bit. A burn, even if it's small, hurts a lot, so your head starts thinking more about the burnt finger on the other hand and starts forgetting about the itching on the hand that isn't there. It would be better to stick a finger from the rubber hand in the flame, that wouldn't hurt. But it doesn't work and, besides, in no time at all I'd have to buy myself a new one. Then what would

I tell my mother? She's due to retire this year, and we barely survive on the salary she receives as a caretaker. I get a small disability living allowance, they should put it up, it's hardly anything. But anyway, a little is better than nothing. We manage. One shouldn't be afraid of pain. Pain is like everything else, something that's there. The question is: who's in control? Who controls who: does the pain control you, or do you control the pain? That's the rub of the matter. Positively. It's nice if you can control the pain. There are times it even gives you pleasure. Listen, I'll give you an example. This is an example. We will carry out an experiment. Take a jug with half a litre of wine. Or beer, better, that makes you want to pee more. Beer is also called 'diuretic', apparently that means it makes you want to go to the toilet. But you can hardly go into a bar and ask for a diuretic, they won't understand you. People's level of information is low. So take a jug with half a litre of beer. Then drink the lot, all the way down. Wait for the need to present itself. Wait until you really need to go. And when the need is greatest, I mean when you're really bursting, that's when we start the experiment. It's a question of holding on, holding on. Holding on for as long as you can. Think of something else, whistle, talk about something, but hold on. Until you really can't hold on any longer or you'll explode. Then, when your bladder is about to burst asunder, take the half-litre jug you drank from and pee into it. You'll soon see how pleasurable this is. This is extremely pleasurable. A great delight. The more you hold on and suffer, the more pleasurable it is to pass water. The funny thing is when you urinate, by which I mean pee, you can't exactly tell if it's nice or painful, isn't that funny? So, to enjoy something, you have to have had a bad time first. In other words – this is what I think – there is no enjoyment without work, no pleasure without pain. Positively. That's a fairly scientific experiment that is within the reach of any human being. So it seems. I don't have much involvement with women, not much, to tell the truth. Though most years I do manage to get my end away. But since, on the whole, I don't take pleasure in women, well, from time to time I do something like this to give my body a beating, to experience another sensation, so to speak. The point is, as anyone who carries out this experiment on liquids will be able to ascertain, you never pee the same amount of liquid you drank. Never. A little part of it remains inside. However hard you pee, a little part remains inside. There's always a bit of wear and tear. Always. It's as if we were to affirm that nothing is immune. Nothing is free, you always have to pay the price. For example, you drink half a litre, but what comes out is less. The company siphons off its share of the profits. I'd like to write a technical book with all my inventions and experiments. I reckon it would help people to learn how to live. Not to be happy, I wouldn't go that far, why deceive people if you don't stand to make anything? If you're going to make something, then I can understand it but, otherwise, what's the point? Life doesn't have a lot of happiness, and one never knows what the best course of action is. One never knows which course of action is more appropriate: whether to sit quiet and endure the attacks and things that rain down on you, or whether to go after life, confront things head on, calamities and what not, so you can overcome them. That's the question. To be or not to be, so to speak. That's what happened to me, I never opted for one course or the other. And once you start pondering things, that's bad. Because, instead of making up your mind, you start thinking, turning things over in your mind, whether it's better to be or not to be, and in the end you are not. That's what happens. That's what happened to me, I didn't make up my mind and now I am not. OK then, when it comes to being, obviously I am here. It's me, in a manner of speaking, I think. But what I mean is I could have been lots of things, lots of people even, but I let myself go, I didn't make up my mind and, by the time you realize, the bell has already tolled. Time has passed, the fight is over. That's what happened to me. That's why I'd say that life is a dream, by the time you realize, the alarm has already gone off, the dream is over, and you're off to the potato field. To sprout potatoes. Positively. All we who are made of flesh are nothing but grass, all our merits are like the flowers of the field. The grass dries up, the flower withers. That's it, down to a T. What I read most are technical books and DIY magazines: *Popular Mechanics*, *Do It Yourself*, *Exercises in Self-Hatred*, *Manual of Self-Harm*, *Handmade*... I don't know, there's a whole load of them. I also have this collection of *Reader's Digest* from the year 1964, it's an American magazine that talks a bit about everything. I know it off by heart. The odd novel, eh. And stories. And then there's Rosalía, Rosalía de Castro's poetry. Rosalía is the tops.

The absolute tops. You see, the women in this country are the tops. They may even be a little over the top, if I may venture an opinion. That's something I haven't delved into yet, I'll have to think about it and see if I can write something in my notebook. But anyway, they're the tops. You bet they are. Take a look at Rosalía de Castro or María Castaña. Or La Belle Otero. Or my mother, who raised her whole family. OK, her husband helped a little, but not very much, you see, drink doesn't let you. What would have happened to us all had it not been for my mother? Mothers are the tops. If you haven't got one, that's a real loss. Though some don't know when to stop, love can kill, a lot of love can smother somebody. There are those who can't get on in life if their mother's not with them. My sisters reckon that's the case with me. I can't say, maybe a bit, though there are far worse cases. Just take a look at Paulino, this guy from my district. When his mother died, he went crazy. All right, he was already a little backward but, when his mother died, he went stir-crazy. Doolally. A mother can finish you off. Fathers can be real bastards. Sometimes they're real bastards. That didn't happen to me – I never quite worked out the question of my father, and besides Xosé was always very peace-loving – but I know a lot of cases that would send a shiver down your spine. Some beat their children so much I'm amazed they don't kill them when they grow up. Or at least return the favour. No, what they do, to get it off their chests, is hand the beating they received down to their children. That's how it goes. Beat one another as I have beaten you, says the Lord Almighty. There are some real bastards out there. Crikey, what a life. I always say that life is a real bummer. Life is a task they impose on you. Positively. But as I was saying, fathers can be real bastards, but mothers also know how to stick the spanner in the works. There are times a mother stops her son – normally this happens with men – stops her son fully growing up. Becoming a man. It's as if you were handicapped and can't manage for yourself. As if a part of you had been pared off. Anyway, there you go, mothers give a lot of love and affection, but sometimes they go overboard. Not my mother, she's very understanding. She's an admirable woman. To an extent, this is what happened with Galicia, there must be lots of women in these parts, the country is like one of those mothers. Men here are never fully grown. I mean it's not as if we're not like other men, I don't know if you can understand me. But it seems we're all a little lacking in initiative, so to speak. Not individually, individually we're like the rest, even more, sometimes. But, put together, we're not worth all that much, we don't seem able to lift our heads. That said, you'll tell me what you think is to be expected of a city like Santiago, which was built for the sake of a dead man buried under all that stone. What can you expect of a country that came into being for that reason? Really. That said, it's a way of living like any other, right? Everybody lives the best they can. Everyone is the way he is, isn't he? That said, with women, there's no telling, am I right or not? Women are the power brokers. You bet they are. You see, women only think with their heads. What I mean is that men have two heads, the one upstairs and the one downstairs, so to speak. The problem is men think with both of them. Were they to think only with the one upstairs, everything would be fine. But they start thinking with the one downstairs, and that's when everything goes to the dogs, as you might expect. By which I mean that the result is not always positive. When that little twitcher downstairs starts having its own thoughts, that's when you have to be firm and get rid of its thoughts before you go crazy or burst. Women are not like that. Women only think with the upper head. Another thing is the difference between actions and words. Let me explain. By which I mean the following. So men either do things but are unable to explain themselves, or they talk, saying they're doing something when they're not actually doing anything at all. In this little country of ours, that's more or less the way of things. My case is different. Well, similar to an extent, but different. I think things over, I give free rein to my imagination, let it run free. I am, so to speak, just to give an example, a worker of thoughts. A philosopher. I lack studies, and yet it could be said that I work scientifically. More or less. But back to what I was saying. Women, you see, they have a place for everything. A place for actions, a place for words. They also have all these other places, needless to say. Oh dear, my downstairs head is starting to work. Let me give a pull on this cord. Aw. God dammit. As I was saying. Women need to be talked to. They like to be talked to. They know very well what they want, and what they want is for you to approach them with nicely chosen words. No turning up like an ogre, fill up and leave. They want some manners. Positively. I had this colleague by the name of Aladio, he was so goddam ugly we called him Toad in the Hole. But this Aladio wielded such charm he could woo any girl in front of him. A girl who wasn't for him wasn't for anybody. We would go to a dance, and he would dance magnificently. He would pass those delicate hands of his around their waists – they were like the hands of a seamstress – and start talking to them. This goes there, that goes here. He would then move in, talk further and further into their ear, like he was tickling them with his tongue. And they would let themselves be embraced and laugh out loud. That was it. Aladio was a machine in action. I don't know whether he hypnotized them by talking in their ear. He talked so well they stopped thinking he was ugly. Women are amazing, don't you think? What they want is for you to invest a bit of effort to be with them. That's what happened to me, I never showed enough interest in a woman. So of course... I have two left feet for that kind of thing. When you think about it, they did well. With a woman, you have to be brave and play the game, whisper sweet nothings in her ear. Like in the story of *Ali Baba and the Forty Thieves*, where there was this huge, stone door that concealed a treasure and, if you didn't say what it wanted to hear, then it simply wouldn't open. But as soon as you said what it wanted to hear – 'Open Sesame' – then it let you in. Women are the same. First you have to investigate: what does she want to hear? Then you have to say it. I've written about all this stuff in a notebook called *The Sesame of Love*, which is to say the ways and technical means of hitting on women. I promise you it never fails. Trouble is putting it into practice involves some effort. But don't think words are enough. Uh-uh. The words let you in but, if you want to stay, actions are required. If they see that you are nothing but talk, they'll throw you out. Into the goddam street. To start with, they act all dreamy and so on but, once you realize, they've come down to earth and are after some serious commitment. That, my friend, is when you have to react quickly: you either say yes or you skedaddle. Women are just amazing. You can't laze about with them, you have to be on the alert, otherwise you'll have problems. That said, I have a great deal of admiration and respect for women. The bad thing is they're the door to this life, which is a great misfortune. I mean, who ever asked them to bring us here, if it's a trap? They don't think about that. If they did, they might sit still. Take the example of my sister-in-law Elisa. A son of hers got killed. The young man hooked up with a local gang and got up to all sorts of mischief, and this chap who owned a kiosk, well, he shot him to pieces. The poor thing now has a child with Down's syndrome who spends all day wearing headphones and staring at the TV screen with the sound turned off. When she wants the child to go to the kitchen for dinner, she shows him a video with her pretending to eat. He sees his mother on the television and gets up and leaves. A real tragedy, a proper calamity. They should put that child in one of those special schools, but she says he keeps her company. One has the impression that life is bad because one doesn't remember it could be worse.

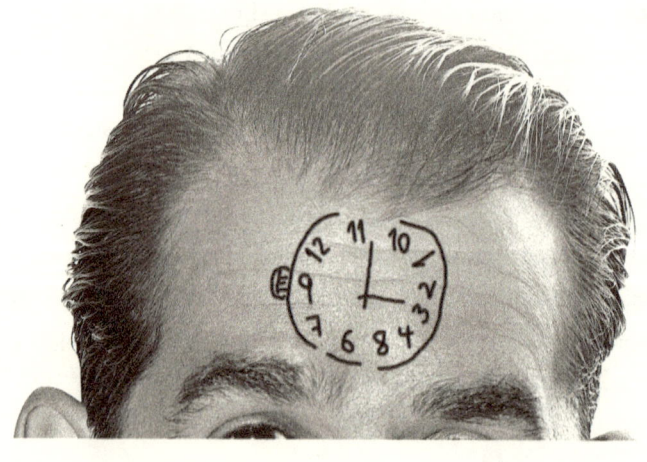

My Name (Chepito)

They call me Chepito, though my real name is José, like my father, who's also called José, though everybody calls him *niño José*. My country is Guatemala, though soon they're going to take me away from here. I don't know, but my mamma and papa sold me for twenty dollars to this gringo man and woman, who are treating me very well, they say nice things to me and give me tasty things to eat. I don't know but, once I've been a month in this house with these people and the other children and have more colour in my cheeks, they're going to come and pick me up a gentleman in dark glasses who doesn't talk very much and take me in a plane to the United States, travelling and seeing all those buildings will be fun, and then they're going to take me to this nice, big hospital and give me an injection so I fall asleep. Then they're going to open me up and take out my intestines, heart, eyes, and give them to the children of people in those parts who are sick and need them, and that way I'll make lots of friends my own age. But when they kill me, something will remain, something small, a word perhaps, that will curse, not forgive. It will curse the names of all the children that receive my parts, of the parents who paid for them and of the country I was taken to. My name, Chepito, will not forgive, it will stay, going round and round and cursing their names. And I will carry on suffering for as long as they last.

Careful (with the Epiphanies)

You have to be careful, you have to be very careful. One lives so complaisantly, as if nothing, there you go, with complete naturalness. Without thinking about things. As if everything happened quite naturally. Or rather as if things happened like that because they had to, because they couldn't happen any other way.

It is better to prolong this state of semi-consciousness as much as possible and let everything continue with an appearance of logic and order, not to shake your head very much and to carry on facing forwards with calm gestures. So long as you don't get vertigo. Anything rather than that. Give yourself repeated blows, keep on making the movement or action you were performing at that moment, sing a familiar song in a very loud voice so you can't hear anything at all, recite a poem or a prayer allatonceatgreatspeed, *The little horse went to peeee at the door of the cooonvent and the local nuuun grabbed hold of its iiinstrument*, everything, everything just so you won't get vertigo. One never knows when it can arise, it appears suddenly and, unless you're quick to react, it traps you and never, never lets go. Well, almost never, there are those who get away. It's the same with this as with everything. But it's better to be careful and to watch out. I just hope such an abyss never, never takes hold inside of us. It's the worst thing that can happen.

To tell the truth, I once suffered from vertigo, it had me in its grasp. Yes siree. It's just good that I was lucky, very lucky, and could get away.

There I was, sitting calmly at the kitchen table. In front of me, I had a plate with a salami sandwich I'd just prepared for myself. I was going to eat it when suddenly I suffered an attack of vertigo.

I was struck by a new vision of everything, a kind of illumination, and saw things apart from myself. My mind was quite alert, time in suspense, I felt sort of hollow inside, as if I were seeing everything for the first time. In front of me, that strange, elongated, soft-looking object at the sides of which appeared something like skins with little red holes, all on top of a white, shining circle. On either side, lying on the smooth surface with painted flowers, some shapes out of which sprouted five long pieces of meat. I examined them closely, they were joined to me by an extension that went up my shirt sleeve. It came from me, they all formed part of me. There was this meat that ended in five slugs. I could see it all in front of me, but it was as if it were all far away. I don't know how long this lasted. It may just have been a moment, a fraction of time, truth is I couldn't tell. But I thought and said, 'If this is part of me, then I can control it,' and I made an effort as if, by staring hard at those pieces of meat, I could hook on to them and then, little by little, pull on a string and they would come, come, until I managed with a great deal of effort to feel them close to me. Once I felt like that, I said to myself, 'Now I'm going to tell this meat to move.' I stared at those little slugs, and finally they moved a little. That was when I said out loud, 'Oh, come off it!' and grabbed the sandwich in both hands and took a large bite. With the taste of the bread and salami, I felt the weight of my body once more, the contact with the air, a sense of distance. Everything was back in its place, and I carried on eating my sandwich. Such is the way of things. Though if I'd had to remain like that for ever... Fuck me.

(From Nano's notebook *On Getting through Life*)

It's Like

crying
  laughing
  walking
  stopping
  eating
  breathing
  sighing
  eating like eating, walking like stopping, singing like dancing, laughing like crying, and eating like eating, walking like singing, this and that, and so on and so forth, to each according to his needs and may St Peter bless what the Lord has given. No. May St Peter bless what God bestows. No. How was it?

  (From Nano's notebook *Concerto for the Left Hand*)

Mother, Dear Mother

He came out of the bathroom with the roar of the water entering the cistern. He closed the door, and the noise all but abated. He passed his damp hands over his chubby, smothered face and black moustache and rubbed his eyes. He grabbed a back issue of *Hello* magazine from the table and collapsed on the synthetic leather sofa. He sighed and sat still with his eyes closed and the magazine in his hand.

Everything was going from bad to worse. The house was in a mess and dirty. If his mother saw how he kept it, she'd punish him. But it wasn't his fault. Adelina the cleaner had stopped coming because she was now too old to climb to the fourth floor without a lift. That was what she had said. Well, he also found it difficult to go up four flights, and yet he had to put up with it. Yes, of course, but he didn't count. Nobody cared about him. He carried on working in the shop for as long as necessary when his mother died, he barely got three days off in which to bury her, three days after that he was back, as if nothing. Because he knew how to fulfil his duty. He did this with everybody, but nobody ever thought about him. He was considerate towards the neighbours and polite with everybody. 'Always act like a human being, son, even if the others don't.' And he was a human being. The previous week, he'd helped the woman in 3-A to carry up a bottle of gas. But who ever helped him, eh? He felt like crying. Whenever he fell to thinking about his bad luck, he felt like crying.

Why shouldn't he cry, then? Of course he should, if he felt like crying. He had every right to cry because he knew how to behave, how to be a human being and fulfil his duty. Of course he did. But he felt very wretched. Why did she have to go and die? He sobbed and made a noise of tears and snot. Why did his mother have to go and die? How much better it would have been if he had died first. He put the magazine on his face and broke into uncontrolled tears and sobs. Why did his mother have to die first? Why hadn't he gone first? She'd always said this: who would look after her child when she was gone? Women nowadays were not the same as before. That's right. Today's women don't know how to look after a man. What will you do when your mother's not here to look after you? Women nowadays only knew how to turn men on. Then, what happens happens, and they protest. Now Adelina was going to retire, and he would be left all alone. He would have liked his mother to be alive so she could see what Adelina was doing. She'd abandoned him with this excuse about being too old to climb the stairs. As if he didn't have to climb them! Even though he was forty, he'd always had a weak pair of lungs. He wondered what his mother would say if she could see Adelina's behaviour. She'd only died a year earlier, and already Adelina was leaving him. So it was hardly surprising the house was in a mess. He wondered what on earth would become of him. Once Adelina retired, he would be left all alone. All alone in the world. Because of his mother. Why did she have to die? I asked her not to die, but she didn't listen.

He took the magazine off his face, pulled a crumpled handkerchief out of his pocket and blew his nose. It would soon be the anniversary of his mother's death, in just over a month's time. He got up and went to the sideboard, took a video marked 'Mother's Final Days' and placed it in the recorder. He switched on the recorder and the TV.

He went to the window and lowered the blinds, letting in only a small amount of light through a gap at the top. He stopped a metre and a half away from the television, hitched up his trousers and kneeled down. He crossed himself and joined his hands in order to pray while gazing at the screen with wide open eyes.

That's the Difficult Part

You think, fool, that the practice of virtue deserves praise and appreciation because in the practice of difficulty is the path of superability, and that's why you look down on me. But I'll tell you that remaining motionless, impassive and distant before the chubby young woman in glasses who has a turn and falls down on the pavement with a chaotic gesture, hurting her knees, laddering her tights, her shoes ending up positioned one next to the other but without a foot inside them as if she'd put them there herself and they hadn't just ended up like that on account of the fall undoubtedly provoked by the advanced stage of pregnancy she finds herself in, that large belly. Watching, motionless, the look of pathetic dizziness on the chubby young woman in glasses who is still on the ground with bewildered eyes, sitting on the pavement, unable to stand up by herself and recover her lost dignity and composure undoubtedly because of the blackout that led to the fall, while along the very same pavement rapidly approaches a group of three ladies three who stare at one, motionless, and then at the other, on the ground and defenceless, ready to reach out to the poor woman in need of assistance. Contemplating, impassive, how the three ladies three rush with agitated movements and trembling gestures first to give air with fluttering waves of the hand, like a fan, to the chubby young woman in glasses who, thanks to the advanced stage of her pregnancy, poor thing, has suffered a dizzy spell and is now sprawled on the pavement surrounded by three ladies who direct an icy, reproving glare at one who watches how, second, they proceed to help her stand up grrrrranting help encouragement and support to the woman who needs it, having recovered a little from the sudden loss of consciousness, and, third, aid the unfortunate woman to direct her spaced out, hesitant footsteps towards a clinic not far from there which belongs to a doctor who's a friend of one of them, no, all of them of course where she will receive the necessary care and attention for a person in her condition. Seeing, distant, how the solicitous trio moves away, taking with them the afflicted, chubby young woman in glasses who has just been through a bad experience owing to the advanced stage of advanced pregnancy she's in and who is now sustained and assisted by those women who occasionally send a look of contempt and reproof in the direction of one who remains motionless, impassive and distant. Now that's the difficult part. You bet it is.

Don't Hit Me

Don't hit me. Father, don't hit me, don't hit me any more. Don't hit me with an open hand, don't hit me with a closed hand. Don't hit me on the head, don't hit me in the face. Don't hit me. Father, don't hit me. Don't beat me with your belt, it makes me cry. Don't hit me, father, don't hit me any more.

Swallow (Love)

Swallow, swallow, you bitch. Nothing. Come on, again. Swallow more. That's it. Nothing, you don't want to. You don't want me today, I see. Not today, you whore. I bet you already did it with someone else. You didn't wait for me. Aah, nothing. Here goes again. Now. No, nothing. Well, I'm not going to let you go. No way. I'm going to give it all to you. Stick it all in. All the way. Even if I get fleeced. Alley-oop, in we go. That's it. No, you don't want to. You don't want this old man, I see. You did before. But I have a hold of you and I'm not going to let go. I won't leave you until you give it to me. I'm going to get it out of you, I'm going to milk you for every last drop, you whore. I'm going to get it all out of you. Even if I'm left without a penny, I'm going to have the 'special'. Come on then. Aaaah, you pig, nothing. Come on, darling, let's see. That's it, have a go with this one, in it goes. Come on then. Nothing. You bitch. Nothing. You're going to leave me with nothing. But I won't let go. No way. You'll give it to me even if you don't want to.

Mater morta

On the screen, mother dressed in a fur coat walks slowly, all hunched up, across the yard of my grandparents' house. She looks at me and waves. 'Hellooo, Paulinoooo. Make me look pretty.' Poor thing, she looks almost finished, she can hardly walk. *Mater divinae gratiae.* And yet, even though she was ill, she still looked pretty. Very pretty. There was no woman her age as pretty as she was. Not even a younger woman. There are no pretty women any more. *Mater purissima.* A decent woman. *Mater castissima. Mater inviolata.* Mother stops in front of the door of my grandparents' house. Zoom, close-up. 'Paulino, promise me, when I'm better, we'll come and fix up my parents' home. We'll have to hire some men to do the painting and retiling.' 'Yes, mother, anything you want. You know I will.' *Mater intemerata.* Poor thing, always worrying. She really loved her parents. *Mater immaculata.* Why did she have to go and die? Nobody loves me any more. She should never have left me. 'Paulinooo, mother's boy!' She blows me a kiss. How pretty she was. How much she loved me. *Mater amabilis.* Nobody ever had a mother like mine. *Mater admirabilis.* On the screen, mother lies motionless in bed. She gazes at the ceiling and has difficulty breathing. She's wearing her pink nightdress. What am I going to do now that she is gone? *Mater boni consilii.* I was luckier than anybody else in this world. I was fortunate to have such a mother. *Mater Creatoris.* She chose me to be her son. *Mater Salvatoris.* What delicate hands the poor thing had. She always looked out for me. *Virgo prudentissima.* She was the best woman and the best mother. *Virgo veneranda.* 'Mother, mother, look at the camera.' She moves her eyes a little and makes as if to smile. Why did she have to die and leave me? *Virgo fidelis.* Her white hair lay combed on the pillow and on either side of her head. *Speculum iustitiae.* I always made sure she was clean and tidy until the last day. She knew this, she kept her wits until the end. *Sedes sapientiae.* I never let Adelina touch her. Cleaning her with a damp towel every day and combing her hair was my business. As she did to me when I was little or got ill. *Causa nostrae laetitiae.* I was happy while she was alive. She made sure I didn't suffer pains. *Vas spirituale.* On the bedside table is a portrait of my father. There was no taking it away from her. *Vas honorabile.* Despite the fact he died a long time ago. Soon after I was born. *Rosa mystica.* But she didn't love him the way she loved me. The camera swerves and the bedside table disappears. Now there's the dressing table with its mirror on the other side. I am reflected in the mirror, holding the camera towards mother. *Turris eburnea.* What will happen to me now that mother isn't here to welcome me back from work? *Domus aurea.* Why did she have to love my father first? She didn't love my father, she never liked men. *Stella matutina.* She was different. Who knows? Perhaps my father never existed. Perhaps she invented him. *Refugium peccatorum.* She cut his photograph out of a magazine. *Consolatrix afflictorum.* She should never have abandoned me. Left me alone. *Regina Angelorum.* She knew Adelina would give up. And there'd be nobody to look after me. *Regina Martyrum.* 'Mother, mother, look this way. Look towards Paulino.' She doesn't look. *Regina Sanctorum omnium.* She should have looked. I wanted a picture of her looking at me as a keepsake. Before she went off. *Regina in caelum assumpta.* When a child asks a mother for something like that, a mother should always do it. *Regina sacratissimi Rosarii.* There's a picture of her gravestone in the cemetery. I ordered it in black marble, the way she liked it. Had it engraved with golden letters. 'María Seijas Padín. 17.11.1992. *Regina Pacis.* Rest In Peace. Your Son, Paulino Seijas Fernández. *Exaudi Nos.*' On the grave, yellow flowers in a glass jar sway in the wind. I should take her some more flowers. A mother doesn't abandon her child. *Miserere nobis.* She was just like the others and left me all alone. To make me cry. *Ora pro nobis.* She always enjoyed teasing me and giving me a fright. *Mater puta.* Had she loved me, she would never have left me like this. *Mater putissima.* She did it so I would suffer, to make me cry. She didn't really love me at all. Who asked her to give birth to me if she was only going to abandon me later on? The image of the grave is cut. On the screen appears the Coyote lighting a fuse that leads to an enormous rock. He's going to blow it to pieces. The Road Runner rushes past. He's going to blow it. No, it doesn't blow. Oh, I get it, the Coyote goes up to see why it hasn't blown, the rock lifts up into the air and then falls back down. The Coyote looks in my direction, ha, ha, he knows it's going to land on top of him. Plaf! Crushed by the rock. Ha, ha.

He stood up and rubbed his knees while staring at the screen. The Coyote was now building a huge bow. Ah, he'd seen this one before. He sat down in an armchair opposite the TV. The Coyote was tying a huge stick of dynamite to a huge arrow. He took out his crumpled handkerchief and wiped it over his face and eyes, his gaze fixed on the screen.

Cuddles

Ah, it's so nice that you love me, so pleasant to feel loved. You don't know how bitter my childhood was. You don't know how populated my childhood was with dead birds and dogs, with afternoons that never arrived and, when they did, barely paid me any attention, with rainy days. You don't know what that was, you have no idea. Shut up, what do you know? When it comes to suffering, me. You don't know how envious I am of that smiling childhood you claim to have had, but love me, love me with cuddles and stroke my hair while I'm talking to you. Love me and say pretty things. Say I'm very good-looking, say I'm very clever, say you love me, say I'm your boy. Love me with affection. Say you love me, but don't spit on me when you talk. Say it with more charm, more feeling. Keep going. That's it. Don't stop.

Winterreise

The winter landscape speaks slowly and ominously. It brings out all that is bad, the worst in me. It peers out of eye sockets and calls, calls. It calls, and sadnesses appear, first one that's bolder than the rest, then all the others in a drove. They open my eyes, explode my eyeballs and eyelids, an enormous hole filling my face. A fucking spring pouring out a bubbling flow of sadness that lands and wets my feet. Wets them, leaving me in disarray.

That's why I've had it up to here with all this winter landscape. All its indecent, mortuary colours, shitty light, the whore that had it, always lifting the shitty stuff to the surface, unearthing the dead. The dead are meant to be left alone. The dead and all that shitty stuff are meant to be kept out of contact with the air. We all have our dead, our shitty stuff. All this winter landscape, it fucks me up. Why does it have to make me like this? Why does it have to hurt me in this way? Could someone tell me? I never know who to complain to in such cases.

TRY WRITING WITH
YOUR LEFT HAND. YOU'LL SEE
IT'S NOT EASY. WHEN YOU'VE

WRITTEN SOMETHING. IT
SEEMS IT'S NOT WORTH
ANYTHING. WE SHOULD
NEVER WRITE WITH OUR
LEFT HAND OR ALWAYS
DO IT WITH ONE OR
THE OTHER.

To One Side

He may have noticed it before and not remembered. Probably as a child when he was on his own in the house and suddenly afraid for no apparent reason. A sensation, a perception you seem to have at a given moment, and then you don't pay any attention to it. Boh, what nonsense, pure imaginings, I thought so, but no, it wasn't, and you carry on with what you were doing, determined to forget this thing that has disturbed you. Yesterday, however, he'd experienced the sensation very clearly.

When he'd got out of the car in the isolated garage, he'd thought there was somebody next to him, he'd quickly turned his head, but nothing. It was a very precise sensation. The same as now.

When he entered the kitchen and opened the fridge, he thought he noticed somebody at his side. He turned his head, but didn't see anybody. For a millisecond, however, he thought he glimpsed a shadow to one side as he turned his eyes. He saw something.

Perhaps it was something or someone that was following him or lived thereabouts. Who knew what might be lurking in the vicinity, something we knew nothing about? Who knew whether there might not be creatures that spied on people and hid themselves from sight? He'd seen it, he'd seen a shadow moving quickly. A shadow or something. What could it have been?

It could have been his guardian angel. Maybe. Perhaps this angel really existed. Always there, keeping an eye on things. He could see it now as he stood there with the fridge door open and a strawberry yoghurt in his hand.

He felt the cold of the strawberry yoghurt on his fingers. Stay still, don't move. Perhaps if he moved his eyes slowly, twisting them as far as possible to one side, he might be able to see it. Slowly does it.

There's Nothing Like Five-A-Side

I laugh and exchange banter with friends we play for a round of drinks or spoof and agree to play a five-a-side match this Saturday at six and carry on cracking jokes at the top of our voices and now we're laughing a lot because we're talking about women. About women. How funny, about women. We laugh a lot, my friends and I, when we talk about women. We all laugh a lot. Almost always when we get together we indulge in banter and play for a round of drinks or spoof and agree to play a five-a-side match this Saturday at six and then carry on cracking jokes at the top of our voices and then laugh a lot because don't ask me how but now we're talking about women. About women. Don't tell me that's not funny, about women. I don't know why but if we're talking about other things, my friends and I, spoof a round of drinks Saturday five-a-side why don't we carry on talking about these things but start shouting even louder and laughing even more because by the time we realize we're talking about women. Can you imagine how funny, about women. My friends and I laugh a lot. We all laugh a lot. And I don't know why but then we all turn very serious and pay and leave as if we've all been invaded by sadness I don't know why. The sadness doesn't last, however, we get home and eat vegetables and the sadness passes we give our wives a peck on the cheek and there you go it's almost gone can you imagine, a bit of everything, like this, and by the time you get to work you're already thinking about meeting up with your mates once more to have a laugh. Ah, how funny, how much we men laugh. But the thing we like best is five-a-side football.

The Fertility of Death

'Youth and green wood, all is smoke,' goes the saying. And an old man like me has to credit this saying. The scepticism of old age is apparent, it certainly is a time of certainties. Certainly.

Against the superficial, arbitrary idea that a human being's plenitude is reached during youth, declines during maturity and deteriorates during old age, I propose the opposite, more realistic idea.

Lactation, infancy, adolescence, youth, maturity and old age are a process of perfection in order to obtain the finished – that is to say, the perfect – article. Complete. The old man in the moment of his death.

Let the contemplation of nature once again provide me with illumination. Nuts guard their fruit under the shell. We guard the shell inside our flesh. But little by little, as the protective flesh matures, it gives its fruit: the shell. That white shell – that skull – is the fruit of our existence.

When that skull is buried, it frees the seed; our death and burial are the requisites for new individuals to be born. They will mature as well.

In the mirror of my bedroom, I see more and more clearly the fruit waiting under that wrinkled skin and can't wait for the day of metamorphosis. I think I am getting ever closer to true knowledge. I don't know whether I shall have the patience to sit still. 'A white layer of frost covered my hair, made me believe I was old already. This filled me with contentment.'

(Manuscripts of Isidro Puga Pena)

Talk, Talk

Talk, talk, feel the words climbing up your throat, epiglottis, tongue, with their powerful arms legs multiple extremities opening and closing opening and closing your mandible and leaping out, explosive, resolved, irrepressible, of your mouth, you wish you hadn't summoned them, but you have, they've come, you've spoken them. Now purse your lips tightly until you have slight wrinkles above and below, deeper wrinkles at the sides, it doesn't matter because now they don't want to come out and, even if they did, it doesn't make any difference because the damage is done and it's better not to say anything you'll say something when you don't want to later, up they'll come again, going crazy, and you won't be aware of them, you'll talk, talk, until one day you've had enough and that day you'll make an effort with masseters and risoriuses and resolutely restrict the movement of those hussies and they'll come up arrive be unable to find a way out and then others will come from behind pushing they can't get out but still others will come scratch you annoyed to begin with then desperate on your palate and tongue and they'll suffocate you take away your breath and you'll die very slowly placing your hand on your throat and opening your mouth wide but it's too late, ah, God dammit, because now they're only as it were little insects lying in agony smothering each other and in this way you won't be able to talk any more. No, God dammit, you won't.

It Was There

Keeping still, I turned my head and eyes very quickly, even painfully, and saw it. It disappeared. But I saw it. It was there, watching me. It vanished, but I caught it first. I try to retain what I have seen, not to forget. I have to retain this valuable moment. If it can, it will try to make me forget, convince me I haven't seen anything. There was no one there. But there was, I saw it.

It had fixed eyes. Eyes that didn't blink. They were clear, as if empty on the inside. But they had strength, the strength that comes from looking. That's because it's always watching me. It'll be watching me right now, powerlessly observing my gestures of concentration, my efforts to remember and etch its figure on my memory. I have to carry on, I have to carry on. Its eyes were meek, but had strength. And yet they were meek. The eyes of a good guardian. The guardian angel.

He had seen his guardian angel. He couldn't believe it. He hadn't believed in his guardian angel since he was little. Kids' stuff, like Father Christmas. He'd stopped believing in that before he stopped believing in God. So then God too must exist. It all existed. All of it. Quick, he had to recall as much as possible, he'd just glimpsed an extremely important mystery. What was it like, what was it like? Around its eyes. He couldn't remember anything around its eyes, just a shadow. Yes, a shadow, a light, blurred shadow. It only has eyes, of course. It doesn't speak. But it has to hear as well, it must have some kind of hearing. The guardian angel.

Dear guardian angel. I caught you out. So it was true, it was true you were there, keeping me company. Protecting me. From what? What the hell did you ever protect me from? Nothing, nobody. All you ever did was watch me. You never did anything other than watch me, spy on me. That's all. When did you ever stand up for me? When I was small, you could have helped me out when the odd bully turned up. You could have helped me out somehow, warned me to get away from there or helped me to overcome him, I don't know. But you didn't. When I was getting the shit kicked out of me, all you did was watch. Watch on whenever my father hit me for some reason. You swine, how little I love you. I'm going to catch you, I'm going to do you in. And then I'll follow you with the one who sent you. I won't forgive him. God knows, I won't.

My Brother

Today I was taken by car for a check-up at hospital. Along the way, from the car, I saw that man who's supposed to be my brother. He was talking to an ice-cream seller. He must be about forty. Or perhaps more, fifty. I can't be sure. He may not even have reached forty and still be in his thirties. I was told he is a little infantile. 'A bit stuck,' said my aunt Lourdes to be exact. I've also been a bit stuck in my life, somewhat immobile, that makes us brothers. I've also heard he drinks. I've always felt the temptation to go over to him and introduce myself, 'How's it going, bro?'

Who knows what he was talking about with the young lad selling ice cream? He didn't seem to be paying too much attention to my brother's animated conversation. I should have approached him when I was still in good health. I probably could have helped him out, I don't think they're flushed with money. Who knows? Perhaps he could have helped me out as well, perhaps he could have taught me so many things I didn't know and didn't know I didn't know until I reached old age.

I should have helped his mother as well. The last time I saw her was about ten years ago. She was standing at the entrance to a building, talking to another woman, dressed in a blue pinafore, holding a brush. I suppose she was the caretaker of that building. I passed in front of the building another couple of times to see if I could see her, but no. Even if I had seen her again, I don't think I would have dared to talk to her. She was still a pretty woman, I could still see in her the young servant I'd fallen in love with. She had filled out and had wrinkles that spoke of years of tiredness, but she still had that serene, determined gaze that once captivated me.

What wouldn't I have given for that child to be mine and not my father's, for that slow boy to be my son and not my brother? Things could have turned out like this if only I'd been more forward. What a wretched life I have led! It seems she may have been happy in her own way, she had other children with another man. My love for her was too pure, too platonic, too sterile. It was the love of a useless child, but it was still love. I think my father was jealous of this love. I think he was impelled by the same instinct that moves us to shoot a bird or pluck a flower. I don't think he really wanted her, she wasn't such a beauty, it was just he saw my simple, sluggish love for her and was jealous of a feeling he couldn't have himself. It wasn't out of love for her, it was out of jealousy towards me. So he could humiliate me once more. I'd have hated him for that, even if he hadn't already been my father.

Although, strictly speaking, all he did was perform his role with implacable naturalness. Now I notice the presence of the gods rooting around my room at the clinic, I feel the hatred peeling away. I keep my sense of resentment, but am no longer able to aim it with hatred at anybody, not even my father. Time kills, but does not allow us to die with dignity, to cling to the hatred we have a right to wield.

I think I shall dedicate a small theatrical piece to my father, which I hope to finish before my hatred, that secret poison, the most personal possession I ever had, vanishes completely. Before all that is left are memories and more vain memories. I think I shall call it *A Revision of Universal Theatre*. Or perhaps *A Revision of Universal History*. It will be a present I can take him when I die and we meet again. Face to face.

(Manuscripts of ISIDRO PUGA PENA)

(A Brief Summary of Universal Theatre)

How dreadful is this place! this is none other but the house
of God, and this is the gate of heaven.
Genesis 28:17

DRAMATIS PERSONAE

HE   (tall, strong, bearded,
wearing a long tunic
like Yahweh, Cronus, Herod...)

SHE   (shorter,
also wearing a long tunic,
sky-blue and white in colour)

GIRL   (Gretel)

BOY   (Hansel)

ONLY SCENE

In the centre of the stage is a house with a staircase that
leads to the front door and continues as a terrace. On the
terrace hang strips of meat and ribs on butcher's hooks.
Also, large knives. Also, ears of maize. On the other side
of the façade is a gallery that looks like a prison, showing
motionless faces, black-and-white or sepia photos of
frightened children.

From the right, a path leads straight to the house. It is
to be supposed that the house is inside a forest.

Enter HE, stage right. SHE follows with a submissive,
eager attitude. HE stops from time to time and declaims
theatrically. SHE follows.

HE (*grave, authoritarian and theatrical, acting out his role*): I know you make offerings, Abraham. Of the finest lambs from your flock. Take now your son, your only son, whom you love, and go to the land of Moriah, and offer him there as a burnt offering on one of the mountains of which I shall tell you.

SHE (*mimicking a child's voice*): Look, the fire and the wood, but where is the lamb for a burnt offering?

HE (*holding back his laughter and imitating a father in agony, though still serene and firm*): My son, God will provide for himself the lamb.

SHE now kneels down, with her hands behind her, and HE raises his arm as if to strike the back of her neck. HE immediately moves to one side and adopts a solemn tone while standing on tiptoe and gazing downwards.

HE: Abraham, Abraham! Do not kill the child. Do not lay your hand on the lad, or do anything to him.

SHE now stands up, and the two of them laugh. HE is more enthusiastic, SHE less so.

SHE: That was a good one.
HE: It certainly was, even if I say so myself.

They advance a couple of steps.

HE: Listen.
SHE: What is it, HE?

HE: You remember Christ? (*HE pretends to be afflicted.*)

SHE: How not? Poor thing!

They look at each other and burst out laughing.

HE (*imitating the suffering of Christ*): Eli, Eli, lama sabachthani? My God, my God, why have you forsaken me?

SHE: Poor thing. I feel sorry for that boy. I really do.

HE: I liked the way he called to me from the cross.

SHE: Your malice knows no limits.

HE (*with pride*): And then I sent Saul to scramble all the doctrines.

SHE: Poor wretch. You told him he would resurrect. I wouldn't like to think what would have happened if he had resurrected and seen the way they tampered with his preaching. Come on, let's go home. We also need the nourishment offered by hearth and bed.

(*SHE starts wearily to climb the stairs, HE follows energetically.*)

HE: Not me. My spirit doesn't flag. All I need is to eat flesh, my appetite knows no bounds. What I don't like is dressing up in carnival costume: as God, Cronus, Moloch... All for a bit of meat.

SHE: You also have to appear the way men dress you.

They each put on a padded dressing gown.

HE: Only the young ones know me, only they see me the way I am. Those young ones are a clever bunch. You bet they are. Only children see me and recognize me. Were there no children...

SHE (*with a distracted look, rubbing her hands*): Yet here's a spot. Out, damned spot! Out, I say!

HE (*staring at her*): Oh dear, the crazy woman is back on her soapbox. Well, it's true. Were it not for the children, I wouldn't know who I was, I have to get dressed up so much. But they know who I am straightaway. 'The Bogeyman, the Bogeyman!' they cry as soon as they see me. They even recognize me in their dreams, 'The Bogeyman, the Bogeyman!'

SHE (*beside herself*): What need we fear who knows it, when none can call our power to account? What, will these hands ne'er be clean?

HE: There's that nutter again, full of remorse. What a nuisance! Were she no use to me, I'd have got rid of her long ago. Silly woman! (*HE shouts at her, but SHE doesn't hear.*) Well, what I like best is eating the little children you give me, as soon as they emerge from your stomach. Nice and tender. Their little legs and arms. (*HE mimics a child's voice.*) 'Don't eat me, Papa Cronus, don't eat me!' 'I'm going to eat you, I'm going to eat you. Yum, yum!' Ha, ha. How stupid can you get!

SHE: There's the smell of the blood still: all the perfumes of Arabia will not sweeten this little hand.

Enter a GIRL and a BOY. The GIRL leads and cares for her brother, who's only little. HE silently watches them approaching his dominion and stares at them from the terrace.

BOY: My legs can't take any more. I'm staying here. I can't walk any further.

GIRL: Your legs hurt. OK, let's rest a bit. (*The GIRL glances from side to side to make sure it's safe.*) But then we'll have to carry on until we get out of this forest.

BOY (*crying*): Why did father and mother run away? Why did they leave us?

GIRL: They didn't leave us, don't cry. It's just we got lost. We lost our way.

BOY: It isn't, it isn't!

HE smacks the other so SHE will wake up from her delirium.

HE: Come on, stupid! Wake up, why don't you? You were back with your old obsessions. Look over there. A couple of kids. Come on, get to work. Look lively!

SHE: Where?

HE: Over there. Get a move on. Bring them to me. Go on, quickly. (*HE pushes her down the stairs, SHE tidies her appearance.*)

SHE: Hello, minikins. Are you lost? My poor darlings!

GIRL: Goodness me, what a pleasant surprise! Could you tell us how to get out of this forest?

SHE: Not to worry, this night you'll sleep in my house. The edge of the forest is far away.

He unhooks an enormous knife on the terrace and slowly starts to sharpen it on a stone.

GIRL: It would help if you could tell us the way. We don't want to be a bother.
SHE: You're not a bother. And, besides, you've arrived just in time for dinner. I'll make you both a nice little bowl of hot chocolate with some doughnuts and honey pancakes. (*To the Boy.*) Would you like that? (*The Boy nods.*) In you go, then.
BOY (*to his sister*): Come on, let's go inside. I'm starving.
GIRL: All right then.

She goes behind them, protecting them with her hands and guiding them towards the house. They walk forwards, staring apprehensively at the house.

SHE: We're all hungry. It's just good you arrived in time for dinner. I've lots of sweet things to eat. You know, even the house is made of chocolate.

The Boy sees the one on the terrace. He is sharpening two enormous knives, one against the other. The Boy stops and makes as if to retrace his footsteps.

GIRL: What is it?

The BOY cannot speak. The words won't come out.

GIRL (*to her*): It's just when he's afraid, he can't get the words out.

SHE: Don't dilly-dally now, it's time for dinner. We'll soon have done with that hunger.

The lights dim and the curtain falls.

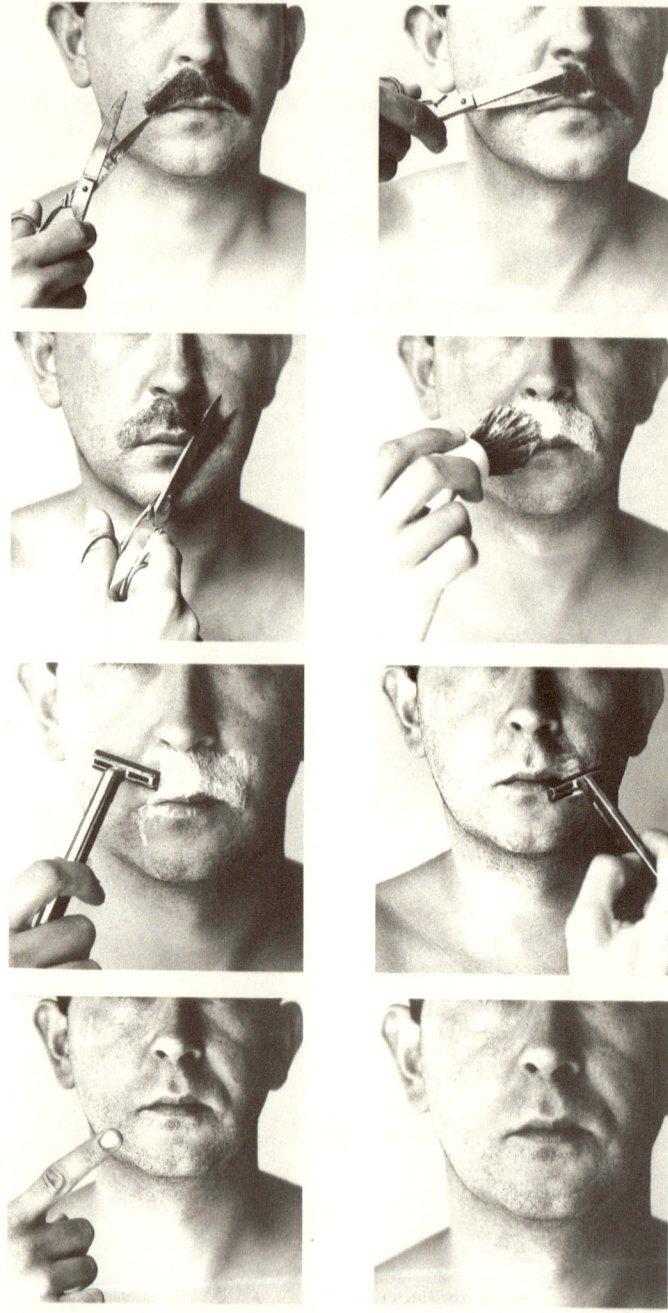

Driver

I'm a driver, you know this already, driving my car, *conduzo o meu coche, sempre conduzo o meu coche,* I head down the road, *é a miña estrada,* this is my journey, *é a miña viaxe,* and zoom past, *conduzo o meu coche,* zooooom.

It'll be dawn soon, *un novo día,* always a new day, *outra vez,* I drive and will see the children on their way to school, *para a escola,* I will cross lands and places, *aquí, acolá e en todas partes,* but the saddest time, *o tempo máis triste,* is the time the children wait, on the lookout, to throw themselves in my way, *ao meu paso,* and the saddest place is the Land of Dead Children, *o País dos nenos mortos,* the saddest land to drive without looking to the sides, *axiña, axiña,* because I'm a driver, driving my car, *conduzo o meu coche, conduzo o meu coche.*

Some day, somewhere, someone will set a trap for me, to avenge the death of their dog or their child that was run over. That day will come. While I'm waiting, I drive my car, *marcho conducindo,* because I'm a driver.

On days like this, when it rains and you start to feel nostalgic, is when I remember my grandparents' house the most. They died already, ooh, where they are now, poor things. Given that I lived there until I was seven. No, until I was six. Or was it nine? Oh, fuck it, I can't remember. The point is, since I lived there the first years of my life, well, that place took hold inside of me and, whenever I feel nostalgic, I remember it. Had someone invented that idea about putting the souls and thoughts of people on chips, which are little devices the size of a breadcrumb, then I could talk to them on a computer. Or at least I could hear them again and keep them company, it must be pretty miserable being dead. Dead children, in particular, make me very sad, whenever I think about the Land of Dead Children, it makes me very depressed. Isn't there some way of giving them a bit of company and warmth? Someone should invent something, but I don't think they have yet. I haven't read about it, anyway, and I keep pretty up to date with technical magazines. The point is my grandparents died and the house was inherited by an uncle and aunt who emigrated to Switzerland. They work in the Nestlé chocolate factory. They're there all year round, but occasionally come here and are making a new house fifty yards from the old one, the one that belonged to my grandparents. They're making it right next to a track. Trouble is my mother doesn't get on so well with this brother on account of the inheritance and so, needless to say, they don't want me going there. But I get nostalgic on account of the rain and have to go there, I start turning round and round in circles and have to go there to get rid of this bug. Otherwise, it's like having a bug gnawing away at my insides. So off I go. I don't have a key any more, so I used to get in through a window at the back. I put it back the way it was, and you wouldn't even have noticed. When I was there, it was something else. It seemed to send the bug to sleep, to calm it down. When I was in that house, if I felt upset, I would be overcome by a wave of tranquillity. I would spend a couple of days there, eating fruit I found in the orchard or stealing some from the neighbour's, that was usually enough. And drinking water from the well. That water, which comes from down below, from inside, is like a consolation. Whenever I came back, I would always bring a bottle with me, just in case. At night, looking at the trees and all those places, I felt a pleasure I'm not sure I could describe. That's something I just don't think I'd be able to write about, I wouldn't find the right scientific method. There, in that calm, I felt a tranquillity that was so big, so big, I wouldn't have the words to describe it. What I felt there is what others feel when they enter a church. But much, much more. I was happy. Trouble is my uncle realized I'd been going, he must have noticed something or a neighbour must have seen, point is – you've got to be hard-hearted to do this – he blocked up the door and windows with bricks and cement. They don't want anything to do with the old house, they've almost finished the new one but, to do me a bad turn, they sealed up the old one. I can't go back. When I got there and saw what they'd done, I felt like tearing down the walls. But I don't want my mother having a run-in with her brother because of me. I've already caused her enough trouble. Sometimes, I go there and take water from the well to bring it here. But I don't have the same tranquillity, the same confidence I had there. And life can be quite hard. One sees so much misfortune in the papers, one suffers so much when one thinks about life's things, one doesn't know what to do. We shouldn't be able to think so much. Sometimes, my head gets so full of words, words hurtling straight through me, I don't know what to do. There are days it's beyond me. But don't pay too much attention, to be quite honest, I'm a bit of a liar. Won't it stop raining? It's about time to leave, it'll soon be nightfall. Apparently tonight there'll be an eclipse of the moon. I don't like eclipses, they appear far too treacherous. They're not natural, like someone getting up to their tricks. I've just seen an old man pushing his handcart, I recognized his face and wondered if it was him. I don't think so, it would be pretty unlucky. But back there he came across my mother and asked after me. He hasn't been back. But one is always afraid one might bump into him. No, it looks like it won't clear.

Here we go, more rubbish. Ouf, it's getting harder and harder to bend over. I've been saying that for at least thirty years. Would you look at this from 5-C? Four bags of rubbish. They don't put out any rubbish for two days, and then put out four together. He may be a doctor, but this is disgusting. In you go. The lift is full, it'll need expanding the way they carry on producing rubbish. I still haven't been to A and B. They don't produce much rubbish. That's because they bring their eggs from the village and don't amass boxes, they buy their milk in plastic bags, which is cheaper and doesn't take up as much space as bottles, their potatoes come from the village as well, I've seen them hauling large sacks of the stuff upstairs. That's why she's so fat. Not him, he plays five-a-side. She stays at home with Irene, getting his dinner ready. They don't read the paper, not like the man in 7-B, the one with the dog and cat, he reads two papers each day. Just to give me more work. When he puts out his bags full of paper, the brute fills the lift. He looks pretty unpleasant too. Come on then. That's it. Down we go. Would you look at this? Travelling among all the neighbours' filth. I wish they could see me, maybe then they wouldn't produce so much rubbish. Uh-uh, what's this? The blasted lift has stopped. That's just what I needed, I was already running a little late. Come on, you stupid lift. No, it doesn't want to. That's just what I needed. Let's ring the bell. See if anybody hears me. And again. I suppose it'll take ages for someone to pass by. Would you believe it? I'll suffocate with the smell of this rubbish. Ugh, it stinks. And there's that bag with shellfish from 6-A. They eat the stuff, I get to smell it. Gaw, it stinks. Get a move on, would you? No. Here goes with the alarm again. No, no one's going to come by. I'll suffocate in all this shit. Nano will get home, and I won't be there. Supper not ready, and I'm not there. Poor thing, what'll happen to him when I'm gone? He can't fend for himself. They say it's all my fault, I spoiled him. Would you believe it? I looked after him like any other child, the way I looked after his sisters. But when I'm gone... Who's he going to hook up with? These things matter. For example, that old guy with the beard and long raincoat that looks like a tunic who came asking after him. He looked like a proper criminal. I told him I had no idea, but I thought I saw him prowling around again today. He reminded me of old Isidro, that son of a bitch, God protect me. Nano's good but, if he keeps bad company, he goes bad. I wanted him to come and pray the rosary with me. When I'm not here, may Our Lady or Our Lord look out for him, he'll be pretty defenceless. His sisters will feed him, no doubt, but he's very delicate, very sensitive. They say I didn't bring him up well. Boh, I cared for him like a son. I wish he'd come and pray the rosary with me, but there's no persuading him. Sometimes he says things in a low voice, muttering away, as if he were praying. 'What's that, Nano?' 'I'm praying the rosary, mother,' he says to annoy me. He's not stupid. Sometimes he's too clever for his own good, but it's his heart that's the ruin of him. Oh goodness, I'm going to die in all this rubbish. Let's give it a try. Crikey! I'm just glad it decided to start working. I was on the verge of suffocating. Come on then, stop here. Let me out so I can breathe a little. Aah, it's a relief not to be there any more.

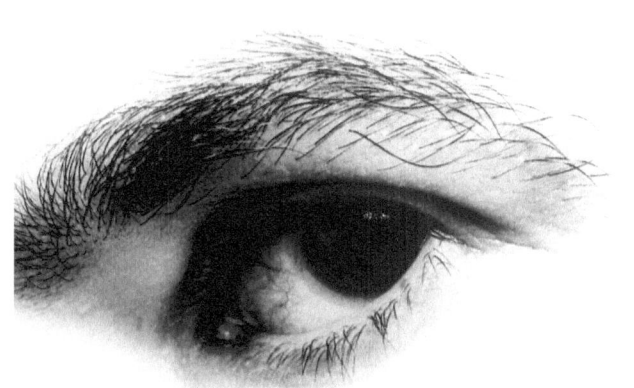

Read more Galician fiction in English from Small Stations Press:

Suso de Toro, POLAROID

One of the most exciting works of literature to have come out of Galicia in the last thirty years, and the first adult-fiction title by Suso de Toro to be made available in the English-language market. There is something startling about this book. With Raymond Carver-like simplicity, the author extracts the commonplace events and ordinary frustrations of life, shedding light on them, exalting them and undermining them at the same time, so that the reader is left in a hiatus, expectant and fulfilled. What goes on here is impossible, outrageous, and yet it happens. A blind man beats and is poisoned by his wife, an aged housemaid tries to breastfeed the baby when the parents are out, a second-hand typewriter insists on typing out its own message, a rapist awaits the family's vengeance while wishing he knew the victim's name, a cash machine flirts with a customer of the bank by making spurious deposits into her account, a jumper turns murderous, a porn model seeks an intimate relationship that isn't confined to the glossy pages of a magazine, a mother loses track of her child, Cain and Abel appear in modern dress, the hero Theseus is driven to question whether he really is a hero or not, a man finds his wife having an affair in the wardrobe… There is something absolutely surprising about these stories that signalled a new direction in post-Franco Galician literature, in a book the author himself described as 'an outburst of fury inspired by punk.'

ISBN 978-954-384-036-6

Miguel-Anxo Murado, ASH WEDNESDAY

In this collection of sixteen short stories by the Galician writer Miguel-Anxo Murado, the reader is taken on a journey through the various rites of passage that make up an individual's life, from the months-old baby who lives in the eternal moment of Nothingness and quickly forgets an argument with his elder brother to the university professor who visits a colleague in Kyoto to see the cherry blossom and before the symbols of impermanence is forced to confront his own terminal illness. Children and adults alike endure extreme situations, from a child who is bullied at school to the Chinese women workers who stay up all night to prepare a handmade suit for the morning. Sailors are rescued at sea; others are cast adrift when their ship sinks, at the mercy of the current. A young man is brought face to face with his late father when surrounded by a mountain blaze; a young girl endeavors to learn the secrets to her sister's radiant beauty. Two boys fall for the same girl; one tries to curry favor with the members of his gang in a story reminiscent of Isaac Babel's *Red Cavalry*, while another searches for the strength inside. All are caught in unexpected situations, elegantly and expertly described, and handed the task of how to react in a book that celebrates the human spirit across barriers of time and language.

ISBN 978-954-384-053-3

Manuel Rivas, THE POTATO EATERS

Sam is a drug addict with a sense of humour. One particular escapade lands him in hospital, where he makes friends with the old man in the adjoining bed and becomes progressively enamoured of the nurse Miss Cowbutt's unsung qualities. In an attempt to wean him off his drug habit, his elder brother, Nico, takes him to the village, Aita, where their grandmother lives, a world far removed from the distractions of modern life, in which even the silence seems animate. He meets up with Gaby the single mother and Dombodán the collector of discarded items. He also becomes acquainted with a slippery customer named 'Sir' who takes refuge in the radio set in the attic. A host of colourful characters – from Tip and Top to the 'relentless lady' – populate this tale, which pits a victim of zero expectations against the haunting traditions of the village.

ISBN 978-954-384-052-6

Miguel Anxo Fernández, **A NICHE FOR MARILYN**

Frank Soutelo is a down-at-heel private detective, the son of Galician immigrants, based in Los Angeles, California. He doesn't get much choice in his assignments and has to take pretty much what's on offer, so when he gets hired and paid an advance of twenty-five thousand dollars, he's understandably pleased, and his secretary even more so. The unusual thing, however, is what he's been asked to do: to recover the body of the actress Marilyn Monroe, which has reputedly gone missing from her grave in Westwood Village Memorial Park Cemetery. Big Frank, as he is known, is about to get drawn into a world that is unfamiliar to him: a world of necrophiliacs, zealous watchmen, uniformed chauffeurs and high-class mansions. The question is will he be able to extricate himself from this situation with his dignity and heart in one piece?

ISBN 978-954-384-051-9

Xurxo Borrazás, VICIOUS

Shakespearean drama set in a Galician context. There is something strikingly postmodern – or Elizabethan – about this novel, in which a man from Laracha, south-west of Coruña, on Galicia's famed Coast of Death, is on the run for committing a multiple murder that shocks the local community and has the priest calling for the razing of the local slums. Chucho Monteiro, who has always been overlooked by his father in favor of his younger brother, Daniel, more pliable, less violent, heads to the port of Coruña in order to effect his escape on the first ship weighing anchor, a ship that will take him not to Stratford, but to Southampton and on. In a fascinating, multi-layered narrative, the author keeps the reader guessing about the murderer's final destination until the very end. Narrative chronology is mixed up, and the veil between author and reader is torn in two, so that we're not sure if we are witnesses or partakers of this narrative. *Vicious* (called *Criminal* in Galician) is Xurxo Borrazás' second and best-known novel, and won him the Spanish Critics' Prize as well as the San Clemente Prize awarded by high-school readers.

ISBN 978-954-384-038-0

For an up-to-date list of our publications, please visit
www.smallstations.com

For more information on Galician literature in English, please visit
www.galicianliterature.gal